AARON ADAMS

POPE'S BOUNTY

Complete and Unabridged

LINFORD
Leicester

First published in Great Britain in 2013 by
Robert Hale Limited
London

First Linford Edition
published 2015
by arrangement with
Robert Hale Limited
London

A catalogue record for this book is available
from the British Library.

ISBN 978–1–4448–2390–5

Published by
F. A. Thorpe (Publishing)
Anstey, Leicestershire

Set by Words & Graphics Ltd.
Anstey, Leicestershire
Printed and bound in Great Britain by
T. J. International Ltd., Padstow, Cornwall

This book is printed on acid-free paper

POPE'S BOUNTY

Jaded gun-for-hire Simeon Pope takes what he thinks will be a routine job. But he finds himself working for both sides of a divided family: the man who wants his errant brother disposed of, and the father who wants his prodigal son safely found . . . Confronted by a bad man, a mad man and a lawman, Pope must find a way to satisfy all his clients, impress the woman he desires — and stay on just the right side of the law.

Prologue

'I'm very satisfied, very satisfied indeed,' said Don Baxter, pouring himself and his guest a large whiskey. They were sitting in the spacious, wood-panelled study in Baxter's house. He was one of the wealthiest ranchers in the area and had no desire to hide that fact. He poured the whiskey from a heavy cut-glass decanter into thick-bottomed glasses. A gold pen and letter-opener were laid neatly on the desk in front of him. The horns of a giant steer, tipped with silver, hung on the wall behind him. 'Yes, Pope,' he continued, 'I'm more than satisfied. Mind you, you did come with the highest recommendation.'

Pope nodded and sipped the whiskey. It was the best he had ever tasted and he moved in the highest circles when he could afford it, or could persuade someone to afford it for him.

'I'm not saying I was immediately convinced by your methods. It went against my principles to pay them squatters anything.'

'It's a mighty wealthy man who can afford principles,' said Pope.

'I am mighty wealthy,' said Baxter.

'It takes a mighty wealthy man with an infinite amount of time to afford principles,' said Pope, evenly. 'A mighty wealthy man with the sense to know it can be cheaper to pay out than hold out, is a man going somewhere in my book.' Pope's flattery worked, Baxter topped up his glass. 'I hope your satisfaction isn't premature,' said Pope, 'I've still got those three remaining boys to remove.'

Baxter leaned back. 'They're an ornery group, I'll grant you. You'll see them off, Pope, one way or another. I don't care what methods you use. I have every faith in you.' He opened a drawer in the ostentatious desk and took out a thick envelope. 'I'm off to

Abilene on business tomorrow, so I'll pay you now,' said the rancher, but he did not hand over the envelope. Instead he squinted his eyes and examined Pope intently. 'I've lived around ignorant folk all my life, and you ain't one of them. You don't just shoot, you think first, and you play a mean game of chess. What makes a class act like you live the life you do?'

Pope said nothing.

'Sure, you don't want to talk about it. The West is full of folks hiding from their own secrets, I'll respect that. I'll pay you for the work you've done, and will do, and it's worth every cent, but how about you staying on? I can easily find work for you. You can put down roots and I'll have a decent chess opponent.' He handed over the envelope. 'There's plenty more where this came from.'

Pope pocketed the envelope and smiled. 'That's a mighty generous offer, Mr Baxter, but I ain't quite ready for putting down roots yet.'

Baxter sighed and nodded. 'Thought that would be your answer. Don't leave it too long though, Pope. None of us is getting any younger. My offer stays open. In the meantime I'll recommend you to anyone who needs your services. The address in Denver still stands?'

'I only work on recommendation, so I thank you. I'm in constant touch with my associates in Denver. It's the best way to contact me.' Pope stood up and offered his hand across the desk. The rancher gripped it and pumped it heartily. 'By the time you return from Abilene, Mr Baxter, your ranch will be free of squatters, I guarantee it.'

* * *

Back in his hotel room Pope counted the money. It was exactly what he'd asked for; he'd never doubted Baxter. The rancher's words had made him think, though. Why did he do what he did? Because he was good at it and it paid well. His debt to Ellen was paid

4

off, though; he'd seen her sons through college, as he said he would. Perhaps he should give some thought to Mr Baxter's advice. He stretched. He was tired, that was all. Once he'd finished this job he'd go to Denver and spend some time with Ellen. Old Brandysnap, his horse, was tired too; he'd retire him up in Colorado and with Baxter's money treat himself to a new mount. And some new clothes. Already he felt better. He packed the last of his belongings into his saddlebags, there would be no need to return once he'd done what he'd been paid for. Stopping only at the telegraph office to let Ellen know his plans, he retrieved his old but willing horse from the livery stable and made his way back to the Baxter ranch.

★　★　★

He passed some of the squatters making their way off the land, their wagons packed high. Most of them acknowledged him with a polite word or two. They knew they were in the wrong and were pleased to have been seen off the land with a minimum of violence and a small wad of cash in their pockets. When word had got around that Mr Baxter had hired a gunman to remove them they had feared for the worst.

Pope nodded to them; they had caused him little bother. One of them actually rode up to him.

'You be careful now, Pope,' he warned. 'Them three boys are no good. They never even tried to work the land, they just stole off the rest of us and spent it on liquor and caused more trouble. Theo's just a kid, he follows the others, but Santos and Grecko are rotten to the core, the pair of them. You'll need to use your gun on them for sure.'

'Thank you, sir,' said Pope, touching the rim of his hat. 'I'll bear that in mind.' The remaining trio had been given the same warnings and induce-ments as the other squatters, if they chose to ignore it, they got what was coming to them.

*   *   *

The boys were more campers than squatters. They certainly hadn't tried to make any form of house, no matter how ramshackle. They had a ripped awning flapping from the side of their wagon, and a few branches bundled together against a hollow in a rock seemed to be their only other shelter. The three young men were sitting around their fire passing a whiskey bottle around when Pope arrived.

The one who appeared to be the eldest, Grecko, stood up. 'We ain't leaving, mister, how many times we gotta tell you before you understand?'

Pope said nothing, but checked that the flap of his jacket was away from his gun.

Santos pulled himself upright now. 'And I'll stay with my friend.'

'And I gotta stay, on account of my

7

pa being buried here. You can't expect me to leave him all alone on the range, can you?' said Grecko.

Pope allowed his eyebrows to rise a little. 'You expect me to believe you had a pa?' he said to Grecko.

Grecko's mouth tightened. 'What you suggesting, mister?'

'I ain't suggesting anything, I'm telling you. You're leaving Mr Baxter's land. Today. That's an order, backed by the law. C'mon fellers, it's not like you're making a living out of this bit of dust. You can hang out and make trouble just about anywhere else you like, so long as it ain't on Mr Baxter's land. Pack up, that won't take long, and head out.'

'What if we don't?' challenged Grecko.

'Then you and your pa will be squatting here for eternity.'

'There's three of us,' said Grecko, softly.

'Try me,' said Pope.

The tips of Gecko's fingers had only

grazed the handle of his gun when the force of Pope's clinical shot sent him flying backwards.

Santos clumsily drew his weapon but didn't fire.

'He was warned,' said Pope. 'You were all warned. Hell, boys, I've no desire to kill you all, but I will if you don't listen to sense.'

Theo was already kicking the fire to death. 'It ain't worth sticking out for a principle, Santos,' he said. 'What have we got here that we can't find anywhere else? Pope's a bad man, but he tells the truth.'

Santos holstered his weapon, but he kept Pope in his sights, his eyes brimming with resentment and suspicion. 'At least let me bury my friend,' he said.

Pope shook his head. 'You show me where his pa's planted and I'll make sure he goes next to him.'

Santos looked at Theo and shrugged his shoulders.

Theo was pushing the tatty awning

into the wagon, he shrugged too. 'He never mentioned his old man till today,' he said.

'I'll bury him where he fell, then,' said Pope.

Santos walked backwards, keeping Pope in view. He mounted his horse, Theo had hitched the remaining horses to the wagon and gee'd them up. Santos followed him, spurring his horse to a gallop and turning round long enough to send a shot towards Pope, which exploded into the dust not far from his feet. Pope didn't even jump. As the figures disappeared over the horizon he relieved Grecko of anything of use or value, which amounted to his weapon and a belt with a fancy buckle, then he hunted around for some stones to cover the body. Grecko had been nasty and a fool, mostly to himself, but Pope would not deny his body some covering.

1

The horse was the most beautiful animal that Scrap had ever seen. Shiny, black as coal, with four white feet and a narrow blaze that ran down its intelligent, bright-eyed face. He ran into the street and followed the animal's progress, glancing up at the rider.

'She's mighty fine-looking,' he said.

The rider looked down, his lined face crinkling further into a grin. 'And you've offended *him* already.'

'Sorry, mister,' said Scrap, reaching up to stroke the animal's neck.

The horse side-stepped slightly and shook his long glossy mane.

'And he ain't too keen on fussing from a stranger,' said the rider, pulling up outside the livery stable.

Scrap held the reins as the man dismounted, and couldn't help tentatively rubbing the velvet-soft muzzle.

The gelding didn't protest too much this time. 'He's just so lovely,' said the boy. He looked back to the man, who was pulling his well-cut jacket straight. 'What's his name, sir?'

The rider reached out and caressed the horse's ear. 'You're evidently an inquisitive boy.' The horse nudged affectionately against his master. 'He's called Baxter,' said the rider. 'He's half-mustang, half-Arabian. I tell you, the sun will stop rising and setting before this game feller gives up.'

The groom came out from the gloom of the stable; his smile slipped when he saw Scrap. 'What you hanging around here for, boy? Don't want you putting off my customers.'

'The kid's just admiring my horse, he's doing no harm. I've a place booked, name of Pope.'

The groom nodded. 'Sure thing, Mr Pope. Mr Willerby told me about you.'

'It's just Pope, I ain't no 'mister'. Nothing but the best for my Baxter, you hear?' He untied his saddle-bags and gave the horse's rump a hefty slap. 'You give him a good curry-combing, he's been ridden hard today.'

The stable hand led Baxter into the stable. All the dust made Pope sneeze, and he reached into his pocket for a handkerchief. As he did so a coin fell on to the ground. Scrap picked it up.

'Here, mister, you dropped a dime,' he said, holding out the coin.

Pope walked away. 'You keep it, kid.'

Scrap ran after him. 'I ain't allowed to beg, mister, they'll run me out of town if I do.'

Pope handed him the saddle-bags. 'Then earn it: carry these.'

★　★　★

Pope had begun to feel depressed the minute he'd entered the dismally named town of Indian Tombs. Going into the saloon made him feel even worse. How many places like this had he been to? There were the usual scruffy tables and chairs, the desultory card game being played by dusty cow-pokes and drifters, ignoring the faded, gaudy women who tried to attract them. The out-of-tune piano was being played badly (though mercifully quietly), and a doglegged staircase led up to the first floor rooms. A wide glass mirror along the back of the bar reflected the miserable scene back to him, doubling his depression. He called over the bartender, ordered a beer and asked Scrap what he would like.

'Whiskey,' said the boy.

Pope laughed and shook his head. 'How old are you, son? I've done many things in my time, but I've stopped short of corrupting a minor, and I ain't about to start now.' He looked at the bartender. 'Give him a sarsaparilla.'

'I can hold my whiskey,' protested Scrap.

'He can,' said the bartender.

'Give him sarsaparilla,' insisted Pope. 'I believe you've got a room booked for me.'

'You must be Mr Pope,' said the

bartender, giving a disgruntled Scrap his drink. 'Room 3, I'll get the keys.'

'Just call me Pope. I'm going to relax and enjoy my drink, no need to hurry.' He walked over to a table and sat down, indicating that Scrap should join him. 'What's your name, son?'

'Scrap.'

Pope took a long swallow. 'That ain't much of a name.'

'Guess I ain't much of a person.'

Pope shrugged. 'How old are you?'

'Sixteen, I reckon,' lied Scrap.

'Thirteen at most,' said Pope.

'More like fourteen. Why'd you ask?'

'Need to establish if you're a liar or not. You are. And twelve, thirteen, sixteen even, that's way too young for whiskey. If you don't beg, what do you do?'

Scrap screwed up his face as if unwilling to say. 'I work here, cleaning and such. My ma was one of the girls, she died a couple of years ago when we had the diphtheria. The other ladies sort of keep an eye on me. What brings

15

you to town, sir?'

Pope's face jerked into a tight smile. 'I'm just here to help someone who's got some accounts to settle.' He finished his drink and handed the glass to Scrap. 'Get this filled up for me, kid.'

Scrap had only just got to the bar when a great shriek came from upstairs. A door on the first floor burst open and out flew a man, his shirt flapping over his undone britches. He was followed by a barely dressed woman brandishing a knife. The man turned and looked over the banister to the bartender. 'This wildcat attacked me,' he shouted, fumbling with the buttons on his pants.

'After what he tried to do to me, I had no choice but to defend myself!' screamed the woman.

'I'd paid you, whore!'

'Not for that, you didn't,' said the girl, lunging at him.

Pope shifted his chair to get a direct view up to the balcony and lifted the flap of his jacket away from the butt of his Colt.

The man and woman were grappling and grunting on the landing. The bartender was running up the stairs, pleading with them to stop. The man had wrested the knife from the woman and now held it against her face.

'If you ain't going to behave like a whore, I'm gonna cut you, so you can't work as one.'

'Leave it, Jack,' pleaded the bartender. 'There's plenty more girls here. Plenty more accommodating ones too. You leave Pearl alone, now, you hear?'

Jack took the knife away from Pearl's face and pointed it at the barman. 'I've paid good US dollars. If I wanna cut her, I'll cut her — ' The knife was blown out of his hand almost before anyone heard the shot. Everyone looked at Pope, who lazily holstered his gun.

'That's mighty fine shooting for a bookkeeper,' exclaimed Scrap.

'Jack,' said Pope, 'you need to check first if you want something that's not on the menu, so to speak. I don't like men who threaten women, you better get out. Pearl, maybe you need to reconsider your profession. Barkeep, my glass needs refilling.'

The bartender instantly ran down the stairs. Jack began to remonstrate, but Pope's redrawn pistol was enough to see him off the premises, shouting, as he stumbled through the door, that Pope should watch his back. Pearl burst into tears and retreated into her room.

Scrap proudly placed Pope's refilled glass on the table and took a seat next to him, pleased to see that everyone was looking. Pope sipped his drink in silence and everyone returned to their former pursuits.

'D'you see much trouble hereabouts?' said Pope eventually.

'Not so much. The man you just whopped is Jack Cannon, foreman up at the Willerby place. None of the girls like him, he's even rougher than the usual types we get round here. And most of them ain't up to much. As for Pearl, she's new and I like her but she cries a lot. I don't think she likes it here. Saturday night can get a bit excitable, but really, not much happens. Where're you from?'

Pope ignored the last question. Nothing the boy said made him feel more favourably about the place. The sooner he did what he'd come to do and left, the better. He looked back at Scrap. 'Go ask the bartender to bring me a bottle of good wine and two fancy glasses with stems.'

Scrap was happy to oblige, as Pope was charismatic and he was proud he had chosen him as an assistant. The bartender came over with the bottle and glasses on a tray.

'What sort of steaks you serve here?' asked Pope.

'Big ones,' said the barkeep.

'What sort of cigars you sell?'

'Big ones.'

Pope stood up and took the bottle and glasses. 'Right, I'll see just how grateful Miss Pearl is feeling towards me, after that I'll have a big steak and cigar. Scrap, take my bags to my room, then we'll say you've earned that dime.'

'If that wine's for Pearl, you might want to consider a cheaper bottle,' suggested the bartender.

'You may sell cheap wine, but there's no such thing as a cheap lady,' said Pope.

★ ★ ★

Scrap was polishing the banister rails the next morning when he saw Pope leave his room and go straight to Pearl's. He didn't close the door behind him, and Scrap edged along the hallway to hear what he was saying.

'You give this letter to Mrs Ellen Holloway, I've put her address on the envelope. You'll have to start at the bottom: cleaning the shop, tidying up after the seamstresses and such like, but if you work hard and show aptitude, Ellen will make you an apprentice. You could have a good career ahead of you. Now it's less than an hour till the stage leaves. Are your bags packed?'

'Almost,' said Pearl, quietly, with a catch in her throat.

Scrap moved to the banister opposite her room, and didn't even pretend to polish.

Pearl was looking up at Pope with an expression of complete adoration on her face. 'Can't I stay here with you?'

Pope reached into his pocket and passed her some banknotes. 'Take that, and no, you can't stay with me. A town like this is no good for a young lady like you. You'll have far more opportunities in Denver. I'll be back in a short while and I'll carry your bags to the stage.'

'If all men were like you I could do this job,' said Pearl.

Pope reached out and gently ran a finger down her cheek. 'Most men you'll meet will be like Jack Cannon. I'm no decent feller either. You're young enough to be my daughter, I should have left you alone last night, but I didn't. Go to Denver and earn yourself an honest dollar.' He turned to leave and saw Scrap. 'You got business here?' he asked.

'Cleaning,' said Scrap, redoubling his efforts on the woodwork.

There was the sound of voices coming from the saloon, followed by footsteps clattering on the stairs. Pope smiled as he was confronted by a woman, past the first flush of youth, sure enough, but still good-looking enough to please him. She was wearing a calf-length split skirt, the sort some women wear for riding, with a thick blouse and jacket. Her handshake was firm, her hands hard and calloused.

'Leah Willerby,' she said. 'I believe you're the man by the name of Pope.' She looked into the room behind him. 'Is that Pearl?'

The girl nodded.

Leah pushed past Pope and thrust ten dollars into the girl's hand. 'Make sure you're on the stage. It leaves in less than an hour.'

'Yes, Miss Willerby,' gasped Pearl.

'Nathaniel,' said Leah to Scrap. 'Go to the general store and load my supplies on to the wagon. There's a candy-stick in it for you.'

Scrap scowled. 'I'd rather have money,' he moaned.

'Which you'd spend on whiskey. Now go.' She gently clipped his ear and he ran off. 'Pope, I need to speak with you,' she said, and Pope obediently followed her down the stairs.

'You've made a bad enemy in Jack Cannon,' she said over her shoulder. 'Oh, I can see by your expression you think him nothing more than a simple cowpoke. He's not. He's the foreman at our ranch. He's persuaded my father and brother he's indispensable. He's not, but that doesn't change the fact they let him do pretty much as he wants. He's got two sons, both equally puffed up with pride and as vicious as their father.

'You humiliated him yesterday. In front of everyone in the saloon. In front of the girl. They plan to come into town tonight, use and abuse Pearl in the worst possible ways and kill you. I have no idea what your business is. Rumour says you're a gunfighter or an accountant.'

She shrugged. 'You're too old for the former and don't look like the latter. So unless the matter is of the most pressing kind, I suggest you leave town.'

Pope took a seat at a table and called for two coffees. He sat upright, broadened his shoulders and allowed an interested smile to curl his lips. At last he'd found something in this dreary town that he liked. And the more she talked, the more he liked her. She was strong, pretty, forthright and intelligent, everything he admired in a woman. Out of necessity he sometimes used someone like Pearl. But by preference he'd rather spend time with someone like Leah. He leaned back in his seat and crossed his arms. 'What do you mean, I'm too old to be a gunfighter?'

She sat next to him and thanked the

bartender for their drinks. 'Gun fighting's a dangerous profession. Most don't make it to thirty, and I reckon you passed that milestone some time ago.'

'I just might be very good.'

'I heard you're a good shot. It's not the same thing.'

'No it's not,' said Pope softly. On impulse he reached out and took her hand. She narrowed her eyes suspiciously, but didn't snatch it away. 'How come a beautiful woman like you has got hard rough hands like this?'

Now she pulled away. 'Drudging,' she said. 'Drudging all day, every day, for my father and brother. Why pay for someone else to do that, when they've got a woman who does it for free?'

He took back her hand and caressed it in both of his. Once again, she was suspicious but did not resist. 'Thank you for warning me about Cannon,' he said. 'I will leave town, but on one condition.'

'Which is?'

'You come with me.'

She swiftly stood up. 'Outrageous! What a ridiculous idea!'

'Then it looks like I'll have to take my chances with Jack Cannon.'

2

Pope enjoyed his breakfast without rushing, and was still in time to see Pearl safely on the stage. He watched Leah Willerby driving off on her wagon, Scrap sat next to her enthusiastically attacking a striped candy-stick. He looked years younger and wholesome. She nodded approval to Pope, and he felt something like pride, good pride, not the vainglorious type. His satisfaction didn't last long though. A hard hand thumped on his shoulder and he jumped with surprise, and shame, that he had allowed himself to be so off guard.

'You've turned out to be something of a disappointment, Pope,' said a gruff voice.

Pope took a step back and fingered the reassuring butt of his pistol before turning to look at his accuser. 'Do I know you?' he said blandly.

'I'm the man that's paying you.'

'Pleased to meet you, Mr Willerby,' said Pope.

'Let's talk,' said Willerby, and Pope followed him back into the saloon. The bartender most respectfully showed them to a small room and soon provided them with coffee and whiskey.

'This is my office in town,' said Willerby.

Pope said nothing, nor did he help himself to either drink, though his companion did both.

'You come with some high recommendation from Mr Baxter in Abilene,' said Willerby. 'Apparently you sorted out the problem he had with squatters with efficiency, imagination and, shall we say, the minimum of bother. But since you've been here, you've offended my best man, Jack Cannon, and drawn attention to yourself. I'm unsure whether to proceed with you or not.'

Other than the fact he'd decided he'd like to see a deal more of Leah Willerby,

Pope wasn't bothered if he was hired or not. 'Your man, Cannon, needs to learn how to behave, if you don't want him drawing attention to himself,' he said.

Willerby snorted. 'Jack's a good man. You had no business taking the girl's part.'

Pope said nothing, but poured himself a coffee.

Willerby sighed. 'My business is pressing, though. Is it true you deal with things? Things that other men shy away from.'

'I help folk out, for a price,' said Pope.

'I need help, sure enough,' said Willerby, leaning over the table. 'And as there ain't no one in town I can turn to, it looks like I'm stuck with you.' He sighed deeply. 'My name's Shadrak Willerby, everyone calls me Shady. Me and my pa, Ham Willerby, run a spread to the north west of here. It's a big enough ranch, and if you put the work in, and I do, it brings in a living. I'm not my pa's eldest, though. That's my brother, Hezekiah, Haze. Now Haze, he never cared for hard work, or the ranch. He reckoned he was better than that. Reckoned he was some sort of artist. He persuaded my pa to give him his due, so he could go to Paris or somewhere fancy, and learn this art thing.'

Pope leaned back in his chair, pulled a cigarillo from his top pocket, and struck a match from the stand in the middle of the table.

Willerby continued. 'So no one's heard from Haze for years, well maybe my sister, though she don't count and God knows she's reason enough to hate him. Then I sees my pa go all misty-eyed over a letter he gets one day. He wouldn't tell me nothing, but I found it and read it. Seems things ain't worked out too well for big brother, he needs a bit more cash.' Willerby's fist slammed into the table top. 'Well I ain't having it! He's had his share, and I know what comes next, he'll be back. I ain't having it! I've given my all to the ranch. I'm the one been out in all weathers and at all times, tending my herd. Haze ain't having any of it!'

Pope held up his hand. 'Steady on, feller,' he said. 'Apart from opening it to find yourselves some fancy names, don't you folk read the Good Book? If you did you'd know how this is going to end. Your brother's coming back with his tail between his legs, your father will forgive him, and you, you learn to live with that or you'll get eaten up with envy and resentment, and be the biggest loser of them all.'

'That's exactly how it *ain't* going to end,' said Shady, 'because you're going to find my brother, and one way or another, and frankly I don't care which way as long as it's permanent, Haze ain't never returning. Mr Baxter couldn't recommend you more highly. 'No fuss, no bother, no conscience, just business,' that's what he said. I'm prepared to pay you good hard US dollars, Pope, if you'll do business with me.'

Pope stubbed out his smoke. 'Where

did the letter come from?'

'New Orleans, I've written it down.' Shady ferreted in his pocket and passed Pope a tatty scrap of paper.

Pope nodded. 'New Orleans is a mighty long way from here. Why do you think your brother will come back?'

'You can tell by my writing I ain't no scholar,' said Shady, 'but I'm sure Haze said in his letter he was making his way back home. I can't risk it, Pope. I can't risk Pa seeing him. You got to stop him.'

Pope frowned. 'I charge expenses. If I go to New Orleans, and I think I may have to, that ain't going to come cheap.'

'Anything,' said Shady. 'I'll take out a bank loan. Anything to stop Haze taking what's mine.'

'Very well,' said Pope. 'You've a deal, Mr Willerby. I'll explain my terms, then we'll shake on it.'

★   ★   ★

Pope had retired to his room and was studying his maps for the best route south east, when there was a knock on the door.

'Mr Willerby to see you,' said the bartender.

Wondering if Shady had reconsidered what was going to be an expensive undertaking, Pope followed the bartender to the small room, where he had previously met Willerby, and was surprised to see an older man sitting in the place where Shady had earlier sat.

'You're the man goes by the name of Pope?' he said, indicating Pope should take a seat. 'You here on any sort of business?'

Pope lit a cigarillo. 'Not especially.'

'Can't see how anyone would turn up at Indian Tombs without reason.'

Pope narrowed his eyes. 'You seem to know my name, all I've been told is that you're Mr Willerby.'

'Ham Willerby, I own the biggest spread round these parts. Last year we drove the herd down to Abilene. Met a rancher there who couldn't talk more highly of you — '

'Baxter,' said Pope under his breath.

'The same,' said Ham.

Pope had appreciated the money Mr Baxter had paid him, which had more than covered the price of the horse that bore his name, and had been happy to let the rancher recommend him, though perhaps he had been a little too adulatory in his praise.

'I've got myself a situation,' continued the grizzled old man. 'I need help, nothing I can ask family for.' He passed Pope a crumpled sheet of paper. 'I've got two sons. Shady, he's my mainstay on the ranch, I couldn't do without him, that's for sure. And there's Haze, my eldest. You ever meet someone who burns so bright, it's just an honour to be with them? That was my Haze. Handsome, clever, so artistic. I don't know how a rough man like me made such a creature but I did. He left, years ago, with, if not my blessing, then with my understanding.

'Last year, out of the blue I got a letter. Not that one.' He pointed to the paper he had given Pope. 'The earlier one was from New Orleans. Things hadn't worked out so well, he needed a loan, so he said: he meant a gift, to get back on his feet and I was happy to oblige. Since then I've sent money here and there. But always, he's getting closer. Look, he tells me to send money to the bank at Festival Ridge, that's less than fifty miles from here. But he sounds ill; the writing is poor, far worse than the first letters he sent me. Find him, Pope, bring him back to me, I'll make it worth your while. I'll speak to the manager and settle up your bill here, and at the livery stable for a start.'

'No, no,' said Pope, hoping he didn't sound too hasty. 'That's not how it works. If I undertake this for you, it's just between the two of us. No one else knows. Once the job is done, I let you know the cost and you pay me cash money.'

'You trust me?'

Pope narrowed his eyes. 'I trust nobody, but I always get paid.'

Ham shifted nervously. 'Do we shake on this or anything?'

'No,' said Pope. 'Leave this to me. I've a good, strong, fast horse. I should be able to report back from Festival Ridge by the end of the week. Just do one thing.'

'What's that?'

'I'll be staying the night here, keep Jack Cannon out of town, eh?'

'Why?' Old man Willerby had clearly not heard of the events of the day before.

'We had a bit of a disagreement, that's all.'

Ham shrugged. 'Jack's my best man. He comes and goes as he pleases. If you can't deal with him, you're not the man that I heard of.'

'Fair enough,' said Pope.

⋆   ⋆   ⋆

Pope returned to his room and poured himself the last glass of wine from the bottle he'd shared with Pearl the evening before. He sighed deeply, but not without slight satisfaction. If he could work for both the Willerbys without either father or son suspecting, it would be pleasing. And finding a solution that solved their conflicting problems was a puzzle he would enjoy. He cared nothing for their ranch and whether it ended up under the owner-ship of Haze or Shady. What he did care about was Leah Willerby and her work-roughened hands. And as for Jack Cannon, well he had no real fight with the man, and, though he thoroughly disliked him, he certainly had no desire to be harmed or to jeopardize his work by taking him on. The sensible thing to do was to leave for Festival Ridge immediately. If it meant a night under the stars, it wouldn't be the first or last time, and though not as comfortable as the saloon, it seemed preferable to having a showdown with Cannon. He drained his glass, threw a couple of items of clothing into his saddle-bags and went downstairs. He instructed the bartender to hold his room for him. Shady Willerby was propping up the bar. He immediately got up and followed Pope out.

'You off to New Orleans already?' he asked.

'Shh,' said Pope, softly. 'I like to keep dealings with my clients strictly confidential, so no talking in the street, eh?'

Shady looked around. 'No one can hear.'

'That's as well,' said Pope. 'I've information your brother may be a deal closer to Indian Tombs than New Orleans. I'm off to see if that's true. I'll report back to you in less than a week.'

Shady frowned. 'How'd you find that out?'

'Contacts. Confidential contacts. Leave everything to me.'

Shady let out a long breath. 'Maybe you're as impressive as Mr Baxter said.'

Pope said nothing and headed for the livery stable.

* * *

Baxter made no secret of his pleasure at being saddled. Less than a day confined to a stable and he was beginning to play up. All in all Pope considered his decision to travel immediately a good one. Nor was he surprised when Scrap breathlessly ran after him as he and Baxter left town.

'You're not off already!' the boy exclaimed.

'Reckon I'll be back,' said Pope.

'Where you going?'

Pope chuckled, and leaned down. 'Scrap, Nathaniel, whatever your name is, take a bit of advice. Don't ask so many questions. I know you're naturally curious, but it's getting a bit annoying now.'

Scrap snorted as Pope gee'd up Baxter and they cantered out of town. Pope hadn't gone far when he heard riders galloping behind him. He pulled up his horse and wheeled him round. He groaned: the middle of the three riders was Jack Cannon. The men faced each other.

'Shady Willerby asked me to back off,' said Jack.

'I'm leaving town. Whatever you've been told to do, it's nothing to me,' said Pope.

'But it's everything to me,' said Jack. 'I've got a score to settle.'

'You humiliated my pa,' said one of the other men. 'We can't let that go without punishment, can we, brother?'

The other man grunted assent.

'I'm off,' said Pope, turning Baxter.

'No you ain't,' said Jack, pulling his gun.

'I ain't worth murdering,' said Pope.

Jack fired and the shot ripped into Baxter's side. He screamed, reared, then staggered. Pope had no chance of staying mounted and was thrown into the dust. Pure ice-cold anger filled him immediately. He quickly got to his feet, even though he was seeing stars, and pulled his gun, aiming it at Jack but the butt of a pistol slammed into the side of his head, knocking him back to the ground. He had no chance of getting upright now as boots slammed into his back and sides, Jack hammering on his head with his fists. Then there was a second's respite before the men roughly hauled him on to his back. Against the bright blue sky Pope could make out Jack's slavering features as the man loomed over him, knife in hand.

'I draw my knife, I gotta cut something,' he said.

Pope felt no pain, only the warmth of his own blood running down his cheek before another fierce attack with fists and feet sent him mercifully into oblivion.

3

'Don't move, keep still, I'm nearly finished. Nathaniel, you hold his shoulders.'

Pope's sticky eyes half-opened. Leah Willerby's out-of-focus face was so close it was almost touching his. He could feel the warmth of her breath on his cheek, then the pinch of her fingers and the stab of something sharp.

'You're handsome enough to take a scar,' she said.

He felt his flesh pulling, saw the glint of scissors and heard the soft snap as the thread was cut.

'Keep still. Still now, this will hurt.'

Something cold and wet was dabbed on his face and it seared into his wound. He heard someone moaning, and when he realized it was himself he decided to give up for a few more minutes. The next time he awoke Leah was standing at the end of the bed. He was in his room at the saloon. Then he remembered and sat bolt upright, screaming with pain as he did so.

She rushed to his side. 'Steady, steady now,' she said, trying to push him back.

'Baxter!' he gasped.

'He's all right,' she said. 'Like you, he's handsome enough to take a scar. Jack's bullet caught him in the withers, it's just a flesh wound. The farrier's stitched him up. You'll both recover if you rest awhile.'

Pope's throbbing head and nausea caused him to sink back unwillingly on the pillows. 'Jack Cannon aimed for my horse. Can you believe that? I knew the man was a heel. Now I've got to sort him out.'

'You're not sorting anyone,' said Leah, pouring a clear liquid into a glass and holding it to his lips. 'Drink this.'

'What is it?'

'Laudanum.'

'Oh, no! I'll not have that.'

She smiled grimly. 'You won't get addicted after one dose, and if you let the pain take over, you'll heal more slowly. Take this, and I'll get you something to eat and drink.' She pushed the glass hard against his lips and he had no choice but to swallow. He felt wretched and weak, which he hated, and he disliked being dictated to, but having Leah so close mitigated his distress. It was only when she had gone that he noticed Scrap was in the room.

'They gave you a pretty good whopping, Pope,' he said needlessly, taking a seat next to him.

'Don't know why they didn't just kill me,' said Pope, closing his eyes and wishing the buzzing in his ears would subside. 'Do me a favour, kid,' he croaked. 'Go down to the livery stable and check on Baxter for me.'

'I'm not to leave this room without Miss Willerby's say-so.'

'Huh? When did she get to be in control of everything?'

'It's 'cause Jack Cannon's threatened

to give me a whopping too,' said Scrap.

Pope tried to raise an eyebrow, a simple action that caused an inordinate amount of pain as the tight stitches stretched. 'Why'd he want to whop you, kid?'

'Dunno,' said Scrap with a shrug.

★   ★   ★

When Leah returned she was keen to speak out on Scrap's behalf. As Pope tentatively sipped some broth she explained that the boy's actions had almost certainly saved him. Scrap had run far enough out of town to see the Cannons threatening Pope. The boy had dashed back to town and persuaded the farrier and the owner of the livery stable to come out with their guns in case there was any trouble. That had been enough to send the Cannons running.

'Though they'd done plenty of damage by then,' she said with a grim smile, 'but at least they didn't break any bones, or kill you.'

Pope grunted. Allowing three idiots like the Cannons to jump him meant he was either not concentrating or he was getting old. Neither was a comfortable thought.

'You might as well leave town as soon as you're able,' said Leah. 'As for Pa and Shady, they'll just have to sort themselves out, if and when Haze returns. You won't get paid, but at least you're alive. I'm sure you'll find another job before long.'

It took him a moment to take in the implications of what she said. 'How long have you known?'

'When I first heard there was a gunman in town, I wondered if you were working for Shady. Then I realized Pa had hired someone to find my brother. I suppose he told you he was last heard of at Festival Ridge.'

Pope swallowed the remainder of the broth. 'So your father and brother both confided in you?'

She laughed. 'They tell me nothing.

They don't notice me either. They talk to each other, they talk to themselves, as if I weren't there. They leave things lying around. I know what's going on. I suspect you're a pretty despicable man, Pope, but that doesn't mean I want to see you come to harm, especially at the hands of a man like Cannon.'

Her words stung him, yet he supposed he was, to a good woman like her, despicable. He didn't want to think, he wanted to sleep, but forced himself to remain alert. 'What are you going to do with the boy?' he said. 'He certainly ain't despicable, and Cannon's after him. He can't stay in this room for ever.'

He heard her sigh. 'No, I must do something about Nathaniel,' she said quietly. 'Give in, Pope, close your eyes, sleep.'

★　★　★

Two days later Pope felt better enough to have a bath and a shave, though the latter proved a painful and difficult experience as his face was still stitched, sore and swollen. He felt better for having made the effort though. He examined his features in the mirror. The right eye was blackened and still not fully open and his left cheek was yellowed by bruising and iodine. Leah's neat stitches reached from his cheek-bone almost to his ear. He splashed on some cologne and put on clean clothes. Beaten and battered though he was, Pope was back.

He met one of the girls on the landing, she stared at him with both curiosity and concern. She also assured him that Scrap was safe, as Miss Willerby had promised to take care of him. Now all he had to do was see how badly Baxter was damaged.

Unfortunately, when he went down-stairs, Jack Cannon was drinking at the bar.

'Here's handsome,' gurgled Cannon into his glass when he saw Pope. 'I can't tell you what a warm feeling it gives me to think every time you look at yourself you'll see the handiwork of Jack Cannon.'

Pope said nothing. Before long Jack Cannon would be feeling the warmth of his lifeblood draining away when Pope shot him. That was for another day, though.

*   *   *

Baxter was on edge. The groom at the livery stable had him tightly tethered so he could not nuzzle the healing wound that was irritating him. He calmed down a little when Pope arrived. The farrier's stitching was nowhere near as good as Leah's, but it would do. Baxter's perfect flesh was marred, but the muscle underneath was undamaged.

'You just gotta be patient, old friend,' whispered Pope, tugging on the horse's ears. 'We both gotta be patient for a while. Reckon I'll still try and sort out the Willerbys and their little situation, and then I'll see to Jack Cannon. Don't you think for a minute, feller, that I'm not going to avenge you, just give me time.' Baxter seemed to nod in approval.

The proprietor of the livery stable brushed aside Pope's thanks for helping him. 'Only doing what was right,' he said. 'That kid Scrap had more to lose than me, he was only armed with a stick. Cannon needs bringing down. He's a bad man, he treats everyone bad, except them no-good sons of his. But he's tangled with you, so he'll get his comeuppance.'

'I'll need to hire a horse while Baxter's recovering,' said Pope.

'Straight away?'

'Yes, and I'd like directions to the Willerby spread.'

* * *

Pope easily found the ranch. If Shady was as hard-working as he said he was, he'd be out on the range, so Pope hoped he wouldn't be confronted by both father and son together, which might prove his undoing. In fact the only Willerby around when he arrived was Leah, which suited him just fine.

'I'm not sure you're ready for a journey yet,' she said, pouring him a cup of coffee.

The ranch house kitchen was clean and comfortable. Pope guessed Leah spent most of her time there. 'Don't you want me to find your brother?' he asked.

She shrugged.

'Shady reckons you had cause to hate Haze.'

She wrinkled her nose. 'Hate? That's a strong word.' She sighed. 'I was keen on a boy from a neighbouring ranch, Haze discovered something about him that meant I wouldn't marry him. Haze did me a favour; better to find out that sort of thing before you're wed.'

Pope said nothing for a while. 'Heard you took care of the kid. What'd you do with him?'

51

'He's here,' said Leah.

Pope slammed down his coffee. 'What a damn fool thing to do!' he exclaimed. 'You've disappointed me, Leah. I can't believe you brought the boy back to Jack Cannon's ranch.'

Leah jumped to her feet. 'This is my ranch, not Cannon's!' she exclaimed angrily. 'And where the hell else could I take him? He never leaves the house without me, I can assure you. It's not ideal, I grant you, but until I can find a better place, it's all I can do.'

Pope silently cursed himself for being hasty, stood next to her and took her hand. 'I'm sorry, I spoke out of turn. I know you'll do the best for the kid. Can I see him?'

She licked her lips and sighed, and though she was still angry she didn't pull away from him, which was something. 'Jack's in town all morning, so I let Nathaniel outside for a while. He is getting bored, I grant you.'

'He must be.' He paused. 'If you've

got a spare horse, do you think he'd like to come to Festival Ridge with me? I owe the boy. Why don't you come too?'

Her eyes shone. 'Pope, that's a wonderful idea! Taking Nathaniel, I mean, not me. I can't leave the ranch. But Nathaniel will go anywhere with you, and, despite the nature of your type of work, I trust you to look after him.'

Her words pleased him. 'Why do you call him Nathaniel?'

'I like it. If I'd had a son that's what I would have called him. Everyone should have a proper Christian name. What's yours?'

'Simeon.'

'Well then, Simeon, you go to the orchard at the back of the house and find Nathaniel. I'll get a horse sorted, get you something to eat and pack you a few supplies.'

Pope moved closer. 'I'd really like to kiss you, Leah,' he said.

She laughed and snatched her hand from his. 'Go get the boy.'

* * *

Scrap was wriggling with excitement by the time they rode away from the ranch. 'Why is it all so secret?' he said.

'Because I don't trust you,' said Pope. 'Now stop twisting about, stop asking questions and start riding hard.' He spurred his horse into a gallop, and heard Scrap shrieking with delight as he followed him.

They rode until only the moon and stars lit the night sky. Pope made a fire and heated up some coffee, and they ate the food that Leah had provided.

'You soft on Miss Willerby?' asked Scrap between mouthfuls.

'You're still asking too many questions,' said Pope.

'I wouldn't blame you if you were,' continued the boy. 'She's not young, but then neither are you. She's good, though. And pretty in her old sort of way, I can see why you'd like her.'

Pope shook his head. 'I've a question

for you. What do you know about Festival Ridge?'

Scrap, who had been lounging against his saddle, sat up. 'Is that where we're headed?'

'Just answer the question.'

'I met a couple of cowpokes from there in the saloon. They were bad! Do you like trouble, Pope? 'Cause that seems to be where you're always heading.'

Pope sighed. 'Out of the mouths . . . ' he muttered to himself.

★   ★   ★

Festival Ridge seemed to be a town with a bit more about it than Indian Tombs. It was bigger for a start: boasting three saloons, a jailhouse, a bank, a general store and a church. The cowpokes Scrap had met might not have been up to much, but the folk of the town, from a cursory look, seemed no better or worse than those from anywhere else. Pope took the horses to the livery stable, and established from the owner that the best of the three saloons was Simpson's.

'I'm looking for a man named Hezekiah Willerby, also known as Haze. Does that ring any bells?' he asked.

The livery man showed no sign of recognition. 'This is a sizeable town, mister; folk come and go. I've never come across a man with a fancy handle like that.'

When asked the same question the owner of Simpson's saloon was less reticent. 'Don't tell me he owes you money, too? If you find the scoundrel I reckon I've got a prior claim to any money you can drag out of him.'

'Let me buy you a drink, friend,' said Pope, most solicitously, 'and we'll compare notes as to our dealings with Mr Hezekiah Willerby.'

Scrap was impressed. Without saying anything of any interest concerning himself, Pope had soon extracted a fair amount of information from Simpson. Haze had arrived in town down and out, but took a job as bartender at the saloon. At first everything had gone well. He said he was an artist and promised to paint a picture of Simpson's wife for him. But Haze had proved dishonest and had his hands in the till as well as surreptitiously drinking the stock.

'And you may want to speak to Doc Maddern,' ended Simpson, 'because Haze spun him a yarn about needing some laudanum on account of the pain of his war wound. But he never paid for it, and stole from his surgery before he left town.'

'Hmm,' said Pope. Ham Willerby thought his son was ill. Off his head on drink and drugs, more like it. 'When did he leave?'

'Only a couple of days ago.'

'On horseback?'

'He had no horse and none was stolen, so I reckon on foot.'

Pope frowned. If Haze was headed back to Indian Tombs they should have passed him on the road.

'He did leave me the painting, though,' said Simpson.

'Any good?' asked Pope, incuriously.

'You make your mind up,' said Simpson, 'though you may not want your young associate to see it.'

'Guess he'll cope,' said Pope.

The painting was propped face to the wall in an outhouse. Simpson swung it round. Pope and Scrap took a step back. A naked woman leaned forward, as if she was about to leap from the canvas, her face distorted with anger, eyes staring, her mouth stretched wide in a silent scream. The paint was thick, daubed in great slabs, the background a mixture of sulphurous yellows and hellish reds.

'Maybe you'd best go back to the bar, Scrap,' said Pope, and with a sulky look the boy obeyed. Pope returned his attention so Simpson. 'I'm sure it doesn't do your good wife any justice.'

'I'd say it was painted from life.'

Pope shifted uncomfortably and indicated that Simpson should turn the

58

picture round. 'It ain't none of my business but are you suggesting Mrs Simpson and Haze were intimate?'

'Sure as hell! That's the job she was doing when I met her, and she's seen no reason to retire since we wed. Only trouble is I didn't realize Haze was paying her with my own takings.'

'May I speak with your wife?'

Simpson shrugged. 'If she's willing to talk to you, it don't bother me. Anything other than words, you make sure you pay.'

'Just words,' Pope assured him.

4

Stella Simpson was lounging on a chaise longue in a room at the back of the bar. She was wearing a thin robe, casually cast over her shoulders, and her underwear was clearly visible beneath. She sat bolt upright when Pope came in.

'What the hell happened to you, mister?' she exclaimed.

'Fell off my horse,' said Pope. 'If you don't mind, Mrs Simpson, I'd like to ask you about Haze Willerby.'

'He owes this man money too,' said Simpson.

'Get back to the bar.' She dismissed her husband with a wave of her hand. She pointed to the sideboard. 'Pour us a drink, mister, I talk better with a glass in my hand.' And talk she did. She had feelings for Haze that went beyond the professional. She referred to him as 'beautiful', 'extraordinary', 'talented'. He had clearly enlivened a life that was not particularly satisfying.

'I've seen the picture,' said Pope. 'It ain't flattering, ma'am. Why would he paint a picture like that, when you were obviously close?'

She held out her glass for a refill. 'Huh! He never let me see the portrait while he was here, but I'll tell you, mister, it's an accurate portrayal of how I feel now he's gone. He was going to take me with him, he said, show me places I'd never even dreamt of. I'd mix with clever, artistic, cultured people. Then he went, without so much as a goodbye. In that one respect he was like every other man.'

'You know he was stealing, drinking and taking laudanum?'

She rolled her eyes as if Pope was a complete fool. 'You've no idea, have you? Someone like Haze is so extraordinary, they can't live in this world, mix with us mortals, unless they have something to dull the pain our idiocy causes them. His mind was so full, his body so active that even full of liquor he was more of a man than any I'd had before.'

'He didn't give you any idea where he was going?'

She downed her drink and shook her head vehemently. 'No, not a breath. One day he was here, the next, gone. He did mention his family had a ranch a few miles to the west. He laughed that no matter what he'd done or did in the future, his pa would always see him right. I don't know if he went there.'

Pope stood up. 'Thank you, ma'am, you've been a help.'

She let the robe slip from her shoulders and her fulsome rouged bosom heaved precariously above her corset. She arched an eyebrow invitingly.

Not even slightly tempted, Pope nodded politely to her and left the room.

* * *

Scrap was not happy about being left out of Pope's meeting with the Simpson woman.

'Stop your whinging, kid,' said Pope. 'I said I would bring you along for the ride and keep you away from Jack Cannon, that's all.'

'You told Mr Simpson I was your associate.'

'It was the first thing that came into my head. It don't mean we're partners. Let's go to the steak-house and eat. I won't leave you out of that.'

Scrap followed him, his eyes down-cast and his hands thrust deep into the pockets of his pants. He had to do something to impress Pope. He had to find out something about Haze Willerby that Pope had not.

*   *   *

After they'd eaten, Pope dispatched Scrap off to the stable to groom the horses, which soured Scrap even further as that was the job of the stable groom, after all. Pope was clearly trying to get rid of him again.

The groom, only a couple of years or so older than Scrap, wasn't happy either. 'Doesn't your man think I'm good enough to tend his horse?' he moaned.

'He's all consumed with finding Haze Willerby; he can't be bothered with me,' said Scrap.

'Haze, the drunken bartender at Simpson's?' queried the boy.

Scrap's brush hovered over the horse's flanks. 'That's the one.'

'Why'd anyone want to find him? 'Cepting he owes money everywhere, my pa included.'

'Your pa?'

'He owns the general store. He was complaining that Haze got him to order some fancy paints or something. Never parted with a cent for them.'

'I've decided you're much better than me at grooming,' said Scrap. He gave the boy the brushes and ran out into the sunshine.

'Have you spoken to Pope yet?' Scrap asked the man at the general store.

'Pope?'

'Big man, with a half-healed scar down his face.'

'Definitely not.'

'He's my boss and he's looking for a man by the name of Haze Willerby.'

The man snorted. 'Him! Does he owe your boss money, too? I haven't the time to go running after disappeared bad debtors, but good luck to the man.'

'So you don't know where Haze went?'

'Surely I don't, and I'm left with a supply of oil paints, which he persuaded me to stock, that no one else is likely to buy.'

Scrap returned to the street, his heels scuffing the ground as he walked. That had been a waste of time. Then he felt a slight tap on his shoulder. He turned round to see a young woman who had been in the store when he was there.

'Did I hear you asking for Haze Willerby?' she said hesitantly, biting her lower lip.

'Yes,' said Scrap. She said nothing more, but neither did she move away. 'It's not about owing money,' continued Scrap; then, not knowing what it *was* about, he decided he'd best furnish her with some explanation. 'My boss, Simeon Pope, is looking for Haze, on account of him being close to Haze's sister and hell bent on marrying her.' It might be the truth after all.

The girl's suspicious expression at once grew more relaxed. 'So your boss is a friend, then?'

'As I said, friend of the family, on account of his friendship with Miss Leah Willerby, of Indian Tombs.' Scrap hoped he wasn't giving away information he shouldn't be, but if Pope couldn't be bothered to tell him the full story he'd have to accept it if things went wrong. 'Do you know what happened to Haze?'

She bit her lip again. 'I don't know,'

she said softly. 'I like Haze, he's a beautiful man, but I know he upset a lot of people here, not paying and stealing and stuff, but he couldn't help it, he's not well.' She reached into her bag and passed Scrap a small square of card. On it was painted a portrait of the woman who stood in front of him. It was softly, kindly executed and very flattering. As unlike the picture of Mrs Simpson as you could imagine.

Scrap returned it to her. 'Could be a photograph of you, ma'am,' he said. 'I suppose it was painted by Haze?'

'Yes.' She looked at the card wistfully before returning it to her bag. 'I'm Sally Maddern, my father is the doctor here. I know he was worried about Haze. He said he was a very sick man and should be in a hospital. Haze came to me and gave me the picture and said he had to go away. He said he'd been to hospitals before and they just made him worse. He said he needed to be alone, to paint and to 'let the demons rip'.'

She frowned. 'I don't really know

what he meant by that. There's some old mine workings to the north of town. Haze used to take me there from time to time; he was fond of the place.' Her cheeks coloured slightly. 'But then my father found out . . . ' She swallowed hard. 'I don't leave town now. Since Haze's been gone I have wondered if that's where he went. I know he loved the light and the ruins of the old workings. As Mr Pope is a friend of the family, I think he should know.'

She paused again, still anxious. 'I hope I've done the right thing. You will tell your boss, won't you? You seem mighty young to be out looking for a man.'

The hell he'd tell Pope. Scrap stretched as tall as he could manage. 'Pope trusts me, and I'm older than I look. Now, if you could give me exact directions to the workings, let's hope we can find Mr Willerby and be of help to him.'

* * *

Scrap found the place easily enough. He pulled his horse to a standstill and surveyed the scene. There were hillocks of rough stone all over the place, a sort of wooden runway, much rotted and broken, that ran from an opening halfway up the hillside and down to the ground surface. To the right of the runway was a tall wooden tower; like the trackway it was decayed: loose pieces of wood and rope flapped in the breeze. To the side of the tower was an assortment of huts and larger wooden buildings. Nailed to the side of one was a notice, but Scrap, unable to read, did not know what it said. He urged his horse a few more yards, then dismounted.

Finding Haze on his own, to get one up on Pope, had seemed such a good idea at the time. Now, alone, surrounded by the vast, abandoned works, he felt very young and vulnerable. He wished he had a gun. What would Pope do? He'd walk straight ahead and call out Haze's name. Scrap did just that.

'Haze, Haze Willerby,' he called, wishing his voice didn't sound quite so high and young. He coughed and deepened his tone. 'Haze Willerby! I gotta message from your sister!' Hell, the man probably wasn't even there. Scrap tied his horse to a hitching rail outside one of the buildings; it still seemed quite robust. He walked up the steps to the door, which creaked on its hinges, but opened. He jumped as some birds flapped up and flew out of the glassless windows; nothing else was there. Likewise the other buildings proved empty. So Haze wasn't hiding out there at all.

Scrap sighed, and pushed his hat up on to the back of his head. There was one last hut, close to the tower. It looked as if it was probably only the latrine, but for the sake of completeness he supposed he'd better check. He clambered over one of the rocky hillocks to get to it, debris clattering noisily down the side as he did so. He couldn't help laughing as he lost his footing and slid down the other side. Breathless and whooping with the thrill now, he made for the narrow shack. There was a boardwalk leading to it, and he began to run along it, arms outstretched for balance.

'No! No!' a voice shouted above him. Scrap looked up. There was a man standing in the opening halfway up the hillside, waving his arms like a madman and screaming. It must be Haze Willerby: he'd found him! He stopped and prepared to shout up to the man, but at that very second there was an almighty snapping and cracking sound. Suddenly Scrap wasn't standing on anything at all.

'No! No!' called the man, and Scrap was screaming now as he descended into darkness.

5

Used to working alone, Pope hardly gave Scrap a second thought as he carried on his enquiries around the town. Wherever he went the answers he got were the same. If anyone knew Haze he more than likely owed them money; yet few bore him any real ill will, and many seemed to have found him fascinating. Even the pastor, who confirmed, as Pope had suspected, that Haze never attended church, told of the many discussions upon spiritual matters he had with the missing man.

Pope was heading for the general store when he saw a brass door plate which read *ALEXANDER MADDERN M.D.* He might as well enquire whether the medic had anything to say.

'You must know that everything between a patient and his doctor is confidential,' said Maddern.

'I'd heard Haze was stealing laudanum from you. I guess that wasn't part of your consultation.'

Maddern smiled sadly and went to the door. 'Sally, bring some tea for me and Mr Pope,' he called down the hallway. He returned to his seat behind his desk. 'No, it wasn't, and you can work out for yourself that Haze wanted more medicine than I was prepared to prescribe for him.'

'And he was drinking too?'

The door opened and a young woman came in and placed a tray on the desk. She looked briefly and quizzically at Pope, but said nothing and left the room. The doctor and Pope sipped their tea and talked generally, but all Pope could infer was that the doctor thought people (that included Haze) were better to have their problems treated medically and not resort to liquor and opium. As for his stealing the laudanum, Maddern seemed more concerned that Haze had been desperate enough to steal it rather than upset at the theft itself.

Having achieved very little, Pope left the doctor to his next patient. A door at the end of the corridor from the doctor's room opened and the woman who had brought the tea waved him into what was a comfortable parlour.

'Are you Simeon Pope?' she asked, closing the door behind them.

He narrowed his eyes. How did she know his Christian name?

'Have you been to the old mine yet?'

'I'm not sure what you're talking about, ma'am.'

'The young boy, your associate, he was asking questions in the general store. I told him about the deserted mine that Haze liked to visit. He said he was going to tell you.'

'I haven't seen the boy for some time, and he certainly hasn't told me anything, ma'am.'

Sally repeated her story.

'Damn fool, damn fool. What's he trying to do, impress me?' muttered Pope angrily.

Sally seemed concerned. 'You think he's gone there alone? I did think he was rather young to be making enquiries. Oh, what have I done? I was so concerned about Haze, I never thought I might be putting that child in danger.'

'Danger?'

'Riding about the range alone.'

Pope smiled grimly. 'Scrap's pretty resourceful. The real danger he's in is the tanning I'm going to give his hide when I catch up with him. Give me the directions, ma'am, and I'll go find him.' He paused in the doorway. 'I was wondering how Haze stole the laudanum from your father. Did you help him?'

'Haze stole nothing,' she said vehemently. 'I gave him what he wanted, laudanum when he needed to calm down, cocaine to allow his thoughts to fly. Father should have seen that Haze was no normal patient, but he just treated him like the arthritic old ranchers he usually sees.'

'Haze must be one hell of a man to get a decent woman like you to procure drugs for his habit.'

She twisted her lips. 'Don't think I haven't paid for what I did. Father will never trust me again. I doubt that, even if I wanted to, he'd ever let me go courting. But I don't care. Haze loved me, in his own way, for a while. No one will ever make me feel that special again.'

'I wish you well, ma'am,' said Pope with a respectful nod.

Even as he spurred his horse out of town, Pope wasn't that concerned, though he felt mighty stupid, and angry with himself for not keeping a closer eye on the boy. Leah had thought better of him, and he'd let her down. Now all he wanted was to get Scrap safely back to her. Haze, Shady, Ham and the rest of them could go hang for all he cared.

⋆　⋆　⋆

Sally Maddern's directions were clear, and soon he found himself confronted by the same ruins Scrap had seen a short while before. The notice, which he read, said 'Land for Sale Contact J Jenkins, Festival Ridge'. He recognized Scrap's horse. He shouted out the boy's name. There was no reply, the only sound being the creaking of the old buildings in the breeze. He shouted again. An emotion almost unknown to him suddenly took hold of him. Fear. If something bad had happened to the boy he'd never be able to face Leah, and that made him afraid.

He heard a tumble of rocks and a man's voice. He instinctively pulled his gun and looked around. He saw a dusty figure running, half-falling down the hillside. The figure stopped for a moment, waved his arms wildly, and seemed to be shouting 'Stay', though the wind snatched away his actual words. Pope dismounted and, still keeping his gun in his hand, headed towards the man.

'Stay!' He definitely heard him this time, and stop he did. He saw now that the man was carrying a rope.

'Scrap!' called out Pope into the air. Still no response from the boy.

The man was almost in front of him now. 'Careful!' he warned. 'There's old workings everywhere.' He stopped, bent double and coughed, a dreadful hollow cough that sounded as if it rattled every rib. When he spat, the spittle that splatted into the dry earth was red.

'You sure ain't well, Haze,' said Pope.

The man pulled himself upright, though one hand gripped his side as if he was holding himself together. 'You anything to do with the boy?' he gasped.

'Where is he?' said Pope.

'Fell down a shaft,' said Haze. 'I dunno if he's dead or alive. Follow me exactly, this place is riddled with holes. I told the boy to stop, but he ignored me.'

Pope holstered his gun and negotiated the rocky path that Haze took, soon they were by the boardwalk, now scarred with ripped lumber and the gap down which Scrap had fallen.

'Careful, friend,' said Haze, as Pope tiptoed over the wood, and knelt down at the side of the hole.

'Scrap, can you hear me, boy? Scrap, c'mon.' Hot acid ripped up Pope's throat and his heart beat fast. He looked up at Haze. 'How long since the kid fell?'

'Not long, twenty minutes at most. I went to get the rope, I was wondering how I was going to lower myself down.'

'You ain't,' said Pope. He returned to Haze, pulled the rope from him and secured it to a heavy metal winding wheel, which was still firmly attached to its housing. 'I'll see what's down here. Get something we can use as a torch. You any idea what's going on under here?'

Haze shook his head. 'Tunnels everywhere, that's all I know.'

Pope tied the other end of the rope round his waist and gingerly lowered himself into the chasm. He waited a while before he swung slightly and was pleased to feel rock against his feet. Gradually he eased his way down the shaft. Then he stopped. What was that? 'Scrap, that you?' he called, sure he'd heard a sob.

'Is that you, Pope?' a watery voice drifted through the darkness.

'Thank you, dear Lord,' whispered Pope, who wasn't normally on speaking terms with the Almighty. Aloud, he spoke to Scrap, 'You hurt, kid?'

'Just my hand, I think.'

The light above the entrance dimmed as Haze leaned over. 'I've got a lantern,' he said. Pope pulled himself back up, took the lamp, then restarted his descent.

At last he could see the white face of Scrap, wide-eyed with fear. Pope's feet touched the ground and he squatted next to the boy, holding the lantern close to him. Apart from a badly swollen hand, he looked all right. 'Thought you must be dead. Why didn't you call out for help, son?' said Pope gently.

'I was frightened of the man. It's Haze, isn't it? He came here to be with demons, so I kept quiet. I was going to try and climb out when he'd gone.'

'Demons?' said Pope. 'Reckon he's been trying to help you. Now can you hold on to me with your good hand and I'll haul you out.'

'How you doing?' Haze's voice echoed down the shaft.

'He's all right. We're coming up. Can you take some strain on the rope?'

Haze's laugh was as hollow as his cough. 'Surely, though it'll probably kill me.'

With Scrap's arms and legs tightly gripping him, Pope grunted with effort and finally reached the top, where Haze relieved him of Scrap and Pope was able to pull himself blinking back into the sunlight.

'Come up to my camp and we'll wash and dress that hand, kid,' said Haze, kindly.

★ ★ ★

Haze had made himself comfortable in the cave, the entrance to which they had seen in the hillside. He had a bed made up on a ledge of rock, there was a campfire surrounded by stones, with a pot suspended over it. Bottles of whiskey and tins of food were neatly stacked up against the wall.

'How'd you get all this stuff here?' asked Pope, for he had seen no horse, or wagon.

'I've been bringing it bit by bit. I've known for a while I've got to get away from Festival Ridge. They all want a piece of me.'

'The money you owe?' suggested Pope, lighting a cigarillo.

Haze put a pan of water over the fire. 'You hurting, son?' He passed Scrap a bottle of whiskey. 'Take a couple of slugs — steady now. If that don't work, I've got something guaranteed to take away the pain.'

Scrap looked up at Pope, who nodded slightly. 'Just two slugs, kid, like the man said.' He looked to Haze. 'My name's Pope, by the way. This kid here is Scrap, though your sister likes to call him Nathaniel.' He thought he'd mention Leah and see what reaction he got.

'How is Leah?' asked Haze as he dipped a cloth into the warm water and gently bathed Scrap's hand. 'How's that feel, Nathaniel?' he asked.

'Sore,' said the boy.

'It ain't broke,' said Haze with a smile. 'At your age bones just bend. Is she still at the ranch, Leah?' he continued without looking up.

'I'll have a slug of that whiskey, if you don't mind.'

'There's glasses over there,' said Haze with a toss of his head, 'if you want to be civilized.'

Pope got up and poured them both a drink. Haze's blotchy complexion did nothing to dim his good looks, but it confirmed to Pope that he was an irredeemable drinker. There was no point trying to keep him off the liquor. 'As you asked, Leah's still at the ranch, waiting hand and foot on your pa and brother.'

'Waste of a damn good woman. I can't imagine why no one's taken her.'

'I aim to,' said Pope, savouring his drink.

Haze looked up from bandaging Scrap's wrist. 'My sister with a gunfighter!' he said scornfully.

Pope was offended. 'Look, Haze, I make no claim to be a saint, not even a regular good man, but gunfighter I ain't.'

Haze shrugged. 'Semantics, Pope. You know what you are, even if you won't admit it to yourself. Has Leah accepted you?'

Pope snorted into his drink. 'Haven't asked yet. I gotta sort you out first.'

Haze was now fashioning a sling from another piece of fabric, while Scrap looked from one man to another, trying to make some sense of what they were saying, even though the whiskey and the shock were making him sleepy.

'So, since I've got a gunfighter or

someone very similar to one after me, I take it someone wants me dead? Is it Leah?' asked Haze. 'I can't believe she'd be so long in taking revenge.' He passed the whiskey bottle to Scrap. 'Two more slugs, Nathaniel, then you'll sleep and sleep's good for healing. Just wish my own advice worked for me.'

Scrap did as he was told. He felt warm and comfortable; if he kept his arm still his hand hardly hurt at all. He didn't want to sleep, though; he wanted to listen to Pope and Haze talking. He had never met anyone like either of these men, and he knew that in some way they were both special.

'You want anything to eat?' Haze asked Pope.

'I got plenty of smokes, you got plenty of whiskey, that'll do me for the night.'

Haze refilled their glasses. 'So, if Leah doesn't want me dead, and for sure my pa doesn't, it must be Shady. But why?'

'Cos he thinks you're going home.'

'I am, eventually. I think you know why.'

Scrap's head jerked as he tried to force himself to keep awake. 'Hey, kid, you've had a hard day, you need to rest. Get comfortable, don't fight it,' said Haze. He let the boy's head sink into his lap and stroked his hair. 'Me and Pope are going to be chawing old man stuff till the early hours, I reckon, so you sleep now.'

Scrap heard the scrape of a match as Pope lit another cigarillo, but despite his best efforts he heard no more.

★   ★   ★

It was a fairly one-sided conversation as Haze mostly talked and Pope mostly listened. It was no hardship, for Haze spoke well, to the point and with humour. Pope began to understand the man he'd been hired to find. Ham Willerby and his wife had clearly no idea what to do with their talented and precocious son. As he grew in awareness Haze realized that with his combination of good looks, wit and charismatic charm he could get pretty much whatever and whoever he wanted. What he certainly didn't want was to be a rancher.

'I wanted to travel more than anything,' he said. 'You've been to Indian Tombs, Pope. Stimulating it ain't.'

Pope nodded a wry agreement to that.

'I wanted to be with interesting, talented people. I wanted to learn. I knew I had a talent for art more than anything. I wanted to be a great artist, I really did. I went to Paris, you know. I was going to study at college, trust me, Pope, I was. But there were so many beautiful people there I got sidetracked, I'll admit it. Though it was the most blissful of diversions imaginable. Wonderful food, conversations that soared, no subjects off limits. And love: love and sensuality everywhere, any time, anywhere, nothing off limits.'

'Then you ran out of money,' said Pope, not having any desire to learn more of Haze's adventures of the flesh.

Haze scowled. 'Money!' he spat. 'So banal, so base, so necessary. You're right, Pope. I ran out of money, and eventually ran out of people prepared to keep me. So, yeah, I had no option but to run back to Daddy. I got a bit sidetracked by New Orleans. Do you know, Pope, there's people there can track their ancestors right back to darkest Africa? Oh, they may well go to church on Sunday, but they get together at night and worship their old gods, in the old ways. Sacrifice, magic, orgies.' His eyes half closed in happy remembrance.

'Trouble with you, Haze,' said Pope, 'is that you ain't got no brakes. Don't it ever occur to you to say 'no'?' He paused. 'What did you do to upset Leah?'

Haze shook his head slowly as if pulling himself back from another world. 'I seduced her fiancé; he'd always had eyes for me more than her.'

Pope downed his whiskey and stood up. 'That was a sick and cruel thing to do,' he snapped, turning his back on Haze and walking to the doorway for some fresh air.

'It would have been someone else if not me,' Haze said. 'He weren't right for her.'

Pope came back into the cave and lay down in the alcove. 'I've heard enough, Haze,' he said, pulling his hat over his face.

Now Haze stood up. 'And I need to work,' he said. He picked up a candle, walked to the rear of the cave and disappeared.

6

Scrap awoke with a start. He was lying on his hand and it was throbbing. He turned over. He was on a bedroll, a thick blanket covering him, alongside the fire. A shaft of golden sunlight was piercing the entrance to the cave. With a slight grunt he pulled himself into a sitting position. He saw that Pope was lying on the bed made up on the shelf, flat on his back, his hat over his face. He occasionally heard a soft, muffled snore. From the rear of the cave came tuneless humming, interspersed with the occasional oath. Scrap got to his feet, and crept along the shaft towards the sounds. The narrow passage opened up to reveal a circular grotto. There were lanterns and candles everywhere, Haze was standing on a tumble of fallen rocks, his brush slashing rhythmically against the wall. Already he had decorated most of the ceiling with thousands of staring eyes, some kindly, some sad, some, frankly, demonic.

'How you feeling, kid?' asked Haze, not looking away from his work.

'My hand still hurts.'

'Will do for a while, son. You'll heal.'

Scrap said nothing as he twisted around, wondering what, if it wasn't demons, possessed a man to do this. He watched Haze working, his brushes dipping into cans of different coloured paints, the random splodges somehow making those strange, staring eyes. Then he realized that what Haze was painting now wasn't strange. 'That's Pope's eyes, ain't it?' he said.

'Pope's got good eyes, don't you think? I mean good, in all senses of the word. Good to paint, grey, with flecks of blue, a hint of green too. Steely but, no matter how hard he tries to disguise it, kind. Good eyes.'

Scrap felt a hand on his shoulder and looked round to see those very eyes, surrounded by Pope's craggy face. 'This is what happens when you live your life fuelled by hard liquor,' he said softly.

Scrap wasn't having that. 'I was born in a saloon, mister; all I know is drunks and I ain't never come across a drunk like Haze before.'

'Don't get sassy, kid,' said Pope, but not unkindly. 'All right, Haze is suffering from hard liquor, strong medicine and a weakness in the brain leading to madness, then.'

'Howdy, Pope, my good man,' called Haze. 'What do you think of my work?' He spun around on his rocky platform. 'This is where it all started. Art. In caves. I've seen works of beauty, painted by those ignorant savages we call Red Indians, that would take your breath away with their magnificence.'

'I'm going to make us all some breakfast,' said Pope. 'While we eat we can talk about what we're going to do.'

'I'm staying here,' said Haze.

'You ain't. I somehow gotta make money out of Ham and Shadrak, and then ride off into happiness with Leah.

I definitely need you for the first two, and since the third is the best thing that can happen to your sister, and you owe her, I reckon you'll be helping me.' He rubbed his hand through his grizzled grey hair. 'I need some fresh air first.'

Haze and Scrap heard the sound of Pope's boots on the stone floor as he headed for the entrance. Then a cough and splutter as he reached the outside. Then they heard gunfire.

★   ★   ★

Pope was crouched just inside the doorway, the barrel of his gun protruding from the side, as he fired off another shot.

Haze retrieved a handgun from his bag and loaded it. 'D'you see who it is?' He crept up next to Pope.

'Someone on horseback. I didn't hang around to make an identification once the lead started flying.' He looked back into the cave. 'You keep out of the way, Scrap, you hear?'

Haze ran across the open doorway; a bullet cracked into the wall.

'Right back, Scrap, go back to where the paintings are,' ordered Pope.

Haze dropped down to the floor, and peeped out. 'Oh no,' he gasped, swiftly pulling himself back to safety.

'You know who it is?' asked Pope.

Haze scuttled to Pope's rifle, which was resting against the wall. He checked it was loaded, then ran with a frightful scream straight to the doorway and emptied the weapon. 'That's stopped you, eh!' he shouted. 'That's told you! That's told you fair and square. If I'd wanted you here, I'd have brought you here, you dumb whore!'

Pope went to Haze's side. He could see a loose horse skittering off, and on the ground a motionless body.

'Stella Simpson,' said Haze. 'The most wretched limpet-like woman you can think of.'

'You killed her,' said Pope, slack-jawed.

'I'd say it was self-defence. Damn fool stupid woman. She's been getting on my nerves for a while now. I don't know why I kept going to her, she weren't even that impressive at what she did. Not compared to the doc's little daughter — now she *was* eager to please . . . '

Pope ran down the rickety wooden slope, Haze calling after him to be careful. The wretched remains were indeed those of Stella Simpson; a bullet from Pope's rifle had pierced her forehead. Pope sat on his haunches and let out a long, agonized sigh. How much more complicated was this affair going to get? By rights he should compel Haze to return to Festival Ridge and let justice take its course. Stella had brought the fight to them, he had no argument there, but Haze's solution had been brutal. No attempt to talk her round had been made. He heard Haze wheezing as he clambered down the walkway.

'A lucky shot,' he said as he saw the corpse. 'I was never a shootist.'

'You could have called to her, you

know, tried to reason,' said Pope.

'You're the hired killer, don't preach to me. A simple-minded, lust-crazed whore aims a gun at you, I reckon, and you know that the only way to stop it is get in there first.'

Pope stood up. 'Killing a woman, though. That ain't right.'

Haze stared at him. 'You're a sentimental old fool, Pope. If Stella'd got as lucky with her shot as I got with mine, you'd be the one staring up at the sky. Go catch her horse, then we'll do the right thing and take her back to town. But I ain't got no bad conscience about what I done.'

'I don't suppose a man who'd seduce his sister's fiancé has got a bad conscience about much, eh?' Pope muttered, before marching off in the direction of the loose horse.

⋆　⋆　⋆

'I'm arresting both of you,' said the sheriff when they returned to Festival

Ridge. There'd been quite a commotion in the town when they arrived and he had bundled them, for their own protection as much as anything else, into to the jailhouse.

'Pope did nothing,' Haze assured the sheriff. 'All I did was protect myself. Come on, Lionel, you know I'm no killer, and Doc Maddern will confirm I'm likely to be dead before the next judge comes to town. Save the county some money. We're moving on anyway, aren't we, Pope?'

'I knew you was trouble the minute I laid eyes on you,' the sheriff said to Pope. 'I should have sent you on your way immediately.'

They could hear Simpson screaming outside and there was banging on the door.

'The townsfolk are going to demand justice. I can't just let you walk away,' said the sheriff to Haze.

' 'Course you can, Lionel,' said Haze smoothly. 'Stella was a working woman and way past her best. Apart from

Simpson, who cares whether she's dead or alive? Last thing anyone wants is some useless trial, that just confirms what we all know happened. All sorts of things get mentioned in the witness box that maybe should have remained private. We're close, Lionel, but the ignorant folk of this town won't understand our special friendship. I'd hate any of them to find out. You go and calm down that angry feller out there, eh? It's your job to keep order, after all. Then me and Pope will just slip away when it's nice and quiet.'

Pope walked into the empty unlocked cell and sat tiredly on the bench that ran alongside the wall. Seeing Leah again and the conclusion of the whole sorry business looked as far away as ever. Haze seemed to have taken over, and as the man was a drug-addled, hair-triggered madman, any chance of a satisfactory ending seemed unlikely.

The sheriff looked uneasy. 'Maybe if I give Simpson Pope to pull apart, that will calm the situation. I see your point,

Haze; I appreciate you trying to protect me. There's no reason for you to stick around.'

Pope let out a long sigh. 'I'm tired, Sheriff,' he said. 'My only involvement here is to find Haze and take him back to his family, I did nothing to that poor woman. Now you and Haze may have some grubby little secret you don't want coming out, but don't forget, just because he's been in your pants, or your pocket book or wherever, it won't stop him killing you, as Stella Simpson would testify if she weren't so stone-cold dead.'

The sheriff was looking completely uncomfortable now, an expression which changed to pure fear as a gunshot cracked into the heavy wooden door to the jailhouse.

'You stop that now, you stop it!' he screamed through one of the shuttered windows. 'I've got the gunfighter Pope under arrest. He'll stand trial for the murder of Stella.'

'I wanna see the murdering bastard,'

they heard Simpson call.

'Only if you leave your gun outside.'

'I ain't receiving visitors,' said Pope.

'And I sure don't want to see Simpson,' said Haze.

'You go to my office, Haze, and climb out through the side window, then,' said the sheriff, 'I gotta do something with Simpson. She may have been a whore but Stella was his wife.'

'Thank you, Lionel,' said Haze, planting a quick kiss on his cheek. 'Sorry to leave you like this, Pope, but, you know, a man's gotta look out for himself. It's a sort of natural justice, I suppose, given you've doubtless killed many and got away with it.'

Pope knew he had to keep calm. Haze's charm was wearing thin now. 'I ain't no murderer,' he muttered. 'Just do one decent thing, Willerby. If you're going to Indian Tombs, take Scrap to Leah, will you. And don't touch him. If you molest that child, I'll know, and I'll kill you.'

Haze slammed the cell door closed

and pressed his face against the bars, his blotchy complexion mottled further by anger. 'I know you ain't no murderer, and, though I know you think I'm a pervert, I would never touch a kid, never. We gotta learn to trust each other, friend.' He disappeared into the sheriff's office.

Lionel was negotiating with Simpson through the window. 'I'm going to take your gun and any other weapon you got, then you can give him a beating if you like.'

Pope leaned back against the wall of the cell, closed his eyes and sighed. He had neither been formally arrested, nor had the sheriff taken his gun from him. He heard a muffled discussion between the sheriff and Simpson. Pope drew his gun. The sheriff opened the door to the cell.

Simpson walked in and screamed. 'He's going to kill me!'

Lionel looked hopelessly on.

'I ain't going to kill you,' said Pope. 'You take a seat over there,' he indicated the bench running along the opposite wall, 'and I'll tell you what happened to your dear wife, God rest her soul.'

★ ★ ★

Despite Simpson's demands that Haze should be charged with the murder of Stella, nothing happened, as Haze had already left town, and the sheriff was reluctant, since only one person was demanding it, to raise a posse to find him.

Pope, still in jail and now gunless, ate his evening meal morosely. It could all have been so very different. He could have got Haze to Indian Tombs, got old man Willerby to see his son, and been paid for that. Then he could have shot Haze — he'd practically be doing the man a favour after all — and relieved Shady of his money. All he'd have had to do then was take the beautiful, willing Leah into his arms. He sighed. His dreams concerning Leah, he knew, were founded on nothing but wishful thinking. He realized, deep down, that she represented his desire for change, for some purpose to his life. He stamped his foot on the floor. 'Hey, Lionel, you got a shot of whiskey or beer? This food's awful hard to swallow.'

'You got water,' said the sheriff's disembodied voice from his office.

Pope put the empty plate on the floor. Damn blast everyone! He'd get the stupid Lionel into his cell; he wouldn't be hard to overpower, escaping would be easy. First thing would be to find out what had happened to Scrap. He'd told the kid to keep well away from him and Haze when they arrived back in Festival Ridge. He just hoped that Haze was good to his word and would take the boy back to Leah. Early hours of the morning, that was when people were most easily disoriented. He'd grab a bit of shut-eye and make his escape later.

He'd only just lain on the bench when the door to the jailhouse opened and Haze swaggered inside. He put his finger to his lips, indicating Pope should be quiet.

'Lionel,' said Haze in a loud whisper, as he headed for the sheriff's office. 'Lionel, I couldn't leave you without saying goodbye.'

Pope rose from the bench and leaned against the cell door. He could hear a muffled conversation, a few grunts, then a short sharp yell and a dull thump. Haze came out with the keys. 'When Lionel comes round I don't know what's going to be sorer, his head or his ass,' he chuckled. 'I told you you could trust me, friend.'

'Scrap?' asked Pope.

'Waiting for us with our horses, just outside town. Don't worry, I looked out for the boy.'

Pope reclaimed his gunbelt and tightened it round his waist. 'What are you, Haze? I reckon I love and hate you in the same measure.'

Haze laughed. 'Now if I had a dollar for every time someone's said that to me, I wouldn't be running home to Daddy with my tail between my legs.'

7

Haze was shaking and jittery by the time they met up with Scrap.

'I just need to attend to a bit of business,' said Haze breathlessly as he foraged in his saddle-bag. 'Fortunately I managed to visit the lovely Sally Maddern.' He smiled happily as he retrieved a glass phial. 'She's seen me all right for a while.'

Pope went over to Scrap and led him a little distance away. If Haze wanted to inject opium, cocaine, or whatever it was, straight into his veins, that was his business, but he didn't want Scrap either to see or get curious. 'You all right, kid?'

'My hand still hurts, but I'm all right, Pope. How did Haze spring you? Was there a gunfight?'

Pope snorted. 'He knocked out the sheriff, who was something of a fool, so it wasn't either clever or dramatic.'

'Oh.' Scrap sounded disappointed.

Haze was leaning against his horse, his eyes closed, his face beautiful in its calm serenity.

Pope went over to him and thumped his shoulder. 'I'm putting some distance between myself and Festival Ridge before I shut my eyes for the night. I suggest you do the same, if you're capable.'

Haze opened his eyes. 'Pope, my friend, I am capable of anything.' He leapt on to his horse. 'Hurry up, cowboys!'

★ ★ ★

Pope reckoned it was about an hour after midnight before they pulled up and made camp in the moonlight. Haze had been erratic during the journey, galloping off, whooping with joy, then slowing down and bursting into tears. Pope made up a bed for him and made him drink whiskey. 'Sleep,

Haze,' he ordered.

Haze gurgled into the bottle. 'I ain't slept for six years, Pope. Tonight ain't going to be no different, 'cept I ain't got my painting to keep me sane.'

Pope took the whiskey bottle from him with his left hand as his right tapped solidly into the side of Haze's head. Haze flopped back on to the bedroll. 'You'll sleep now,' said Pope grimly.

★ ★ ★

Despite his swollen eye, Haze was perky the next morning. 'I knew you were going to be good for me,' he said to Pope as he tucked into his breakfast beans. 'I ain't slept like that for years. No dreams, no demons.' He threw down his empty plate and stretched his arms high above his head. 'I don't need the liquor or the laudanum, you just clock me one every evening and I reckon I'll be a well man within a week.' He sprang to his feet.

'Bedlamite,' said Pope under his breath, as he tidied up their belongings.

'What you saying, dear Popey, Poppy, Pope, my dear, dear, friend?'

'You ain't well, Haze, and you ain't never going to be, but I'll happily knock you into oblivion at regular intervals, if it helps.'

Haze was saddling his horse. 'Popey, Popey, Popey, my dearest friend,' he recited in a sing-song manner.

'Is anyone interested in the plan?' asked Pope, tidying up their pans and kicking dirt on to the fire to kill it.

'What plan?' said Scrap.

'Glad you're listening, son, since you've an important part to play.'

Scrap stood tall, his expression keen. 'You trusting me, Pope?'

'Sure am.' He shot a sly glance at Haze, who was kissing his horse's nose with some passion. 'Though you ain't got much competition.'

Scrap grinned and looked eager. 'What you want me to do?'

'I'm going to make camp just outside

Indian Tombs and the Willerby spread. You ride in and find Leah. But you gotta be careful, boy; you creep in there and make sure Jack Cannon don't see you.'

Scrap nodded. 'I can do that.'

'You sure, now? 'Cause I know anything happens to you, Leah's sure gonna kill me.'

'I can do it, Pope. What do you want me to tell Miss Willerby?'

'Tell her where we are, bring her to us if she wants to see her brother. Tell her if she wants to bring her pa, so be it, but not to tell Shady that Haze has been found. You got that?'

'I got it.'

'And we probably don't need to tell Haze much, either.'

Scrap looked over Pope's shoulder. 'He's coming,' he whispered.

Haze seemed determined to hug Pope, who was equally determined not to be touched. Eventually he allowed Haze to loop his arm over his shoulder, and then led him to his horse and heaved him into the saddle.

'You taking me home, Popey Pope?' asked Haze, laughing.

'Not quite,' said Pope.

* * *

Leah came with Scrap to Pope's camp. The moment he saw her Haze burst into tears, his handsome face crumpled and his rackety, wheezy sobs reached violent proportions. She held him close until he began to calm down.

'I got an illness, sis, deep inside, eating away at me. Doc says I won't last a year.'

She hugged him tighter and soothed him. 'There, there, Haze, you cry if you want.'

And cry he did for some time. Then he sniffed and juddered and pulled himself away from her. He rubbed his nose with the back of his hand and asked Pope for whiskey. 'Years haven't been too unkind to you, sis,' he said. 'You're still a good looking-woman.

Pope thinks so, don't you, Popey Pope?' He snatched the bottle from him and took a deep pull on it. 'What do you think of our lovely Popey Pope?'

Leah smiled slightly. 'Maybe I'm coming round to him, though he should keep a better eye on Nathaniel.'

'I love Popey, and, sis, this is for sure, there's no way I can tempt this one away from you, much as I'd love to, because I do adore my Popey Pope, but he don't care one jot for me.' Haze began to giggle and hugged the bottle in between swigs, singing a nonsense song as he did so.

Leah went over to Pope. 'Thank you for finding him, Simeon,' she said.

'Sorry your brother's in such a state, ma'am. The doc in Festival Ridge reckoned he should be in a hospital.'

She looked back at Haze, who was drawing a picture of Scrap in the ground with a stick. 'I'll look after him.'

Pope stared at the ground. 'Reckoned you'd say that. Do you have no care for yourself, woman?'

She sighed sadly. 'What else can I do?'

'Leave your pa to sort him out. Leah, I got strong feelings for you. It seems to me you've spent your whole life at someone else's beck and call. Let me show you some love, let me give you a better life. Come with me. Come with me tonight. I'll not bother with the money from your pa and Shady. Hell, I'll even let Jack Cannon live. Scrap can go into town and get my horse. Please, just stay here, with me.'

Leah frowned. 'How can running away with a gunfighter make my life any better, Simeon?'

Pope's mouth twisted with anger. 'I ain't a gunfighter,' he said slowly. But she was right: how would being with him help her to a better life? 'I'm going to sort myself, get a spread of my own, I've got money,' he muttered.

She sighed again. 'Sure, Simeon, sure. You get your horse and go away, I'll take Haze back to the ranch.' She bit her lip. 'I'm still not sure what to do about Nathaniel, though. Jack Cannon's still baying for him, and you . . . '

'But you wouldn't want to leave him permanently in the care of a gunfighter, would you?' said Pope bitterly.

'No. I'll take him with me.' She turned to her brother. 'Haze, you rest a while.'

He looked up at her, smiling vacantly, like an innocent child. 'Sure. You're going to make it all right, aren't you, sis?'

Leah held out her hand. 'Thank you again, Simeon. You did the right thing, bringing my brother to me. I wish you all the best, with your sorting out and your ranch and whatever.'

Pope did not take her proffered hand. 'I'm going into town to get Baxter. Put Haze on his horse and come with me; he can rest plenty when you're back at the ranch.'

'I think I know what's best for my brother. We don't need to go into town, we can get straight back home from here. You go, Simeon, or do you want

114

me to pay you? I haven't much, but I guess you've earned it.'

He turned and walked away from her, anger screaming through his whole body.

★   ★   ★

'He's been going crazy,' said the owner of the livery stable, as Baxter nuzzled against Pope while at the same time kicking out a back leg and swishing his tail bad-temperedly.

Pope stroked his horse. The wound had healed and the scar was nowhere near as bad as he feared. He felt his own face. He'd go back to the saloon, freshen up, and pick out his stitches, which were itching furiously. Then he'd ride out to the Willerby spread and kill Jack Cannon. At least that way he'd know Scrap would be safe from the man, and it would be one less worry for Leah. She'd have enough on her plate with Haze and the rest of her family. He looked down at Baxter's wound again, Jack Cannon deserved what was coming to him.

'I'll take him out once I'm cleaned up,' he said to the owner of the livery stable, and headed off to the saloon.

* * *

Pope didn't enquire whether Shady Willerby was still paying his bills; as his room was as he had left it he guessed everything was in order. He lay in the bath, savouring a glass of whiskey, and then, with a slight amount of pain and bleeding, removed the thread that Leah had so neatly put into his face. He supposed he'd better eat before he finished off Jack Cannon, since he certainly shouldn't hang around town after that. While he waited for his meal to be cooked he spent some time with one of the girls. Since Leah had made it patently clear she had no interest in him, he felt no guilt about that, though it didn't cheer him as much as he had hoped it would, either.

Riding Baxter was a pleasure. The horse was frisky and bad-tempered, but as soon as they left the confines of the town Pope eased off the bit and let him have his head. They would have made it to the Willerby spread in record time if Shady hadn't met them halfway.

Shady pulled up his horse. Pope did likewise, though rather more effort was needed.

'You seen Leah recently?' asked Shady. 'I know you've been sniffing round her, dirty dog that you are.'

'I saw her this morning, and I can assure you there's nothing between me and your sister.' Pope stopped. Was Shady suggesting that Leah was missing? Despite having eaten well an hour ago, he felt hollow. 'When did you last see her?'

'This morning. She was talking to that kid Scrap, then she said she was going to get some supplies. Don't know why, she was in town yesterday. It don't

117

normally take her so long.'

'Where's Jack?'

'Other side of the ranch. He's got no quarrel with Leah.'

'He has with Scrap. If he tried to hurt the kid, Leah would sure have intervened. He could have harmed her.'

'No, Jack's nowhere around, I'm telling you. Did you see Leah in town, and what have you found out about Haze?'

'I saw Leah at my camp, just north east of your ranch house. I had Haze with me, and she was going to bring him home.'

Shady's face reddened. 'He's alive? And here? You know that's not what I wanted.'

'Steady on, feller,' said Pope. 'Leah was bringing your brother home to die. He's a sick man and no threat to you and your precious ranch. But if Leah didn't make it back, then I gotta find out where she is.' Pope spurred Baxter on.

Shady followed him. 'Don't you trust

a darn thing Haze tells you!' he shouted after him.

★   ★   ★

Back at the ranch house they found Ham Willerby sitting in front of his open, empty safe, rocking back and forth on his chair, crying. He suddenly looked very old and frail.

'Pa! Pa!' shouted Shady, kneeling in front of him. 'What happened?'

'It's all gone,' spluttered Ham.

'What?' said Pope.

'Two thousand dollars and my claim to the ranch.' Ham looked at Shady. 'We're ruined, son. I can't pay the men. I can't even prove I own the land I'm sitting on.'

Pope frowned. He didn't understand any of this. 'Has someone broken into the ranch house?' he asked.

The old man shook his head, his red rimmed eyes welled up with more tears. 'My safe was opened with my key. Only me and Shady know where it's kept — '

'I stole nothing!' exclaimed Shady. 'Hell, Pa, that would be stealing from myself!'

Ham reached forward and took his son's hand. 'I don't think it was you. I reckon Leah knew where I hid the key. She's gone, hasn't she? Taken her horse, not the wagon like she usually does. She's ruined us, Shady. Why? Why? Why'd she do that?'

Shady held his father tight. 'No, Pa. it ain't Leah. She would never do that. She's as much a part of this ranch as we are.'

Pope took a step back. He needed to get away from there. He needed to think. Had Leah lied to him? He'd certainly believed her when she said she was taking Haze to the ranch. Did she already have the money with her then? Had she done it? He couldn't get the spectre of Jack Cannon out of his mind. Shady thinking he wasn't around meant nothing. Some sixth sense in Pope told him it was time to go. He edged to the door and made his way silently towards

Leah's kitchen. He stopped briefly as he heard a commotion at the front of the house. After a few muffled words and some shouting he heard a loud authoritative voice boom.

'I'm US Marshal Makepeace Cridland and I've a warrant for the arrest of Hezekiah Willerby and Simeon Pope for the murder of Lionel Pike, sheriff of Festival Ridge.'

Pope had heard enough. His heart pumping, he tore through the kitchen and out into the garden. He crept along the wall of the house and peeped around the corner. Baxter knew he was there and flicked his ears forward. Pope saw half a dozen mounted men. Damn it, Cridland must have a posse. He noticed that he had only looped the rein over the hitching rail. He made a soft hissing noise. Baxter flicked his ears again. Pope risked a louder hiss, Baxter shook his head, that was enough to dislodge the rein, and, despite his previous friskiness, he wandered slowly over to Pope. Once round the corner

Pope was on him like a flash and steering him through the orchard. The low fence was easily jumped and Pope was on the open range, Baxter was off like streaked lightning. His heart still pounding and his head throbbing, Pope headed east, hoping the last place Marshal Cridland would think he would go was Festival Ridge.

8

It was dark. Pope and Baxter were both completely spent. They had been walking for some time, and now the horse was faltering, tripping over stones that would normally never bother him. Pope let him come to a halt by a shallow stream, and slithered off him, running his hand along the soaking withers of his faithful mount.

'I've no desire to run you into the ground, Baxter my boy,' said Pope tiredly, loosening the girths and pulling out his whiskey from the saddlebag. 'Let's have a drink.'

Baxter wandered to the stream and put down his head. Pope sank to the ground and leaned against a rock. Whiskey had never tasted this good before. For a moment he felt nothing, only the delicious trickle of the liquid down his throat. He let out a long juddering sigh. He couldn't think, and now that he had sat down he couldn't even move. He tried stretching his legs, but nothing happened. He drank more whiskey. Nothing. Not even the sound of Marshal Cridland's posse, which was something. Now he yawned. One more drink. He pushed the cork firmly back into the bottle. What the hell was going on?

★   ★   ★

The warmth of the early morning sun on his face woke Pope. He was relieved to find that he could move, and pulled himself upright. He was even more relieved to see that, tired as he was, he'd remembered to cork his whiskey the night before, as the bottle was lying on its side on the dusty ground. Baxter had wandered off a short distance and was grazing peacefully. He looked up briefly when he saw Pope moving, but soon returned to his enthusiastic munching. Pope went down to the river, drank, then held his face under the sharp cold water. His wound stung, and he pulled himself away. He decided against making a fire for coffee, instead he rinsed his mouth with whiskey and helped himself to a couple of dry biscuits from his saddle-bag.

He knew his whole opinion of Leah was based on fantasy. He had to accept the fact that she had stolen from her family and she and Haze had disappeared somewhere together. How long had they been plotting? Had she played him like a fiddle? And why had she stolen the old man's claim? What good would that be to either of them?

At least without the marshal on his heels Pope felt he could safely return to the camp where he had left Leah, Haze and Scrap, and see if he could tell from the tracks where they were headed. Or had Jack Cannon simply come across them, done something typically bad, killed them even, then gone back to the ranch house (he probably knew where the safe key was as well), robbed his employers and run away? Why Ham's claim, though?

The more Pope thought about it the stupider it seemed, unless of course, it was simply to cause the old man pain. As Ham had treated Leah, of all his children, the worst, it made it more and more likely she was in some way involved.

Baxter nuzzling his back roused him from his reverie. 'Why'd she do it?' he asked the horse. She'd been desperate to get rid of him at the camp. If she really had intended to return to the ranch, surely they would all have travelled together.

'Why steal the claim, Baxter?' he said again. 'Why'd you need to prove you own something? Something belonging to Ham Willerby.' His mind raced. Ham Willerby, or H Willerby? You need to prove you own land to make out a loan against it. A loan for what? To buy what? Then he saw it in his mind's eye, nailed lopsidedly on the derelict building. 'Land for Sale'. He slapped

Baxter's rump and tightened the girths. 'You weren't there, boy, you didn't see it. But why would anyone want to raise a loan to buy a disused silver mine?' There was no need to return to the camp now. He jumped aboard his horse and spurred him along the trail to the mine.

★   ★   ★

He tied Baxter next to Haze's, Scrap's and Leah's horses. Haze was mad, possibly very bad, certainly dangerous and unpredictable. How had he managed to persuade Leah to go along with his scheme? Pope crept up the rickety wooden stairway and into the cave. Leah was bent over the fire, stirring something in a pot. She looked up as his shadow darkened the doorway, and in that split second of recognition he knew she was pleased to see him. His smile was broad.

She left the fire and went over to

him. 'Simeon,' she said softly. 'You found us.'

'Found you,' he said gently. 'You've got yourself into a mess, Leah. Reckon you'll need me to sort it out.'

She frowned, pushed the pot off the flame and indicated that they should go outside. They walked along a narrow terrace which led up to a flat ridge that looked down on the whole site. She sat on a rock and bit her lip as she surveyed the scene. Pope sat right next to her, and she leaned against him.

'Sorry I lied to you, Simeon,' she said.

'I reckon Haze has that effect on people. He's what you might call a corrupting influence. You should be apologizing to your pa. Losing his money and his ranch is a hard blow for him; it could see him off.'

'Hmm. He knows it's me stolen from him?'

'Who else, Leah? Why'd you do it?'

'I had a letter from Haze a couple of weeks ago. He said he had a way to make back all the money he had from Pa when he left home. He said he'd make us all rich. He and I could go and live out West, San Francisco maybe, and Pa and Shady wouldn't need to work the ranch unless they wanted to. He wanted to make amends for going away. It sounded so plausible, Simeon. All we had to do was raise the money to buy the mine, then he'd reveal the silver seam he'd discovered and we'd sell the place on at a massive profit. He was determined to do it all legal and above board. For once.'

Pope put his arm around her shoulder, and kissed her forehead. She didn't resist and if anything, snuggled closer to him.

'I've been a foolish old woman, haven't I?'

'You ain't old,' he said with a smile. 'Where are Haze and Scrap?'

'In the grotto, Haze is still painting, he likes to talk to Nathaniel.' She let out a long shuddering sigh.

'He paints to hide the silver he's

found?' asked Pope.

'There was a rock fall, it exposed a massive silver seam, so he says. I don't know whether I believe him or not, now.'

'Look at all this,' said Pope, indicating the workings below them. 'You don't abandon a mine like this without tunnelling, blasting, prospecting every last inch to make sure it ain't worth carrying on. Maybe Haze has found a silver seam, but it won't cover any investment you make. If there was still a mother lode here, the valley would be alive with men, alive with hammering and alive with blasting.'

She wrapped her arms around him and let out a soft sob into his chest.

'You still got the money and your pa's claim, Leah?' he asked, and felt her nod. 'Good, that's something. On no account part with them, promise me?' He felt another nod. 'I gotta tell you about another development.'

She looked up at him. 'What?'

'There's a US marshal with the

marvellous name of Makepeace Cridland. Together with his posse he's out to arrest me and Haze for the murder of the sheriff of Festival Ridge. They were at your ranch, and I can't figure why they haven't caught up with me yet.'

She pulled away. 'You didn't kill the sheriff, did you?'

'I surely didn't, and Haze told me he'd only knocked him out. Haze did shoot Stella Simpson because she got on his nerves, though, and I guess I should have made sure he got arrested for that. But he's a dying man, and he's your brother, and I don't deal with the law, so I did nothing.'

'You're right, Haze is a corrupting influence. What are we going to do, Simeon?'

He reached out and cupped her chin in his large, rough hand. 'Don't reckon I'll be able to think straight until I've kissed you, Leah.'

★   ★   ★

Haze threw his paintbrush down, stamped his feet and pummelled his fists into the rock face, such was the extent of his tantrum. 'You promised me, sis. You promised!' he shrieked.

'I indulged you, but I shouldn't have,' said Leah. 'We need to forget this whole nonsense about the mine, and go home.'

'Leave him awhile,' said Pope. 'I can't get any sense from him about the sheriff while he's like this.'

'What about the sheriff?' sniffed Haze.

'Lionel, your friend, he's dead and we're both wanted for his murder. Did you whop him harder than you needed to?'

Haze sobbed. 'I loved Lionel. He was nice to me. It was just a little tap, Pope. I only sent him to sleep so I could spring you. It's all your fault. I hate you, Pope, I wish I'd killed you. I will kill you!' He sprang towards Pope who neatly dodged him, leaving Haze sprawled on the ground.

Pope indicated to Leah that she should follow him and they walked along the shaft back to the entrance to the mine. 'You ain't going to like this, but I suggest we leave Haze and I'll take you back to your pa.'

'I can't,' she said.

'You must. You can't help him, because he can't, or won't be helped. I've gotta see you safe, Leah, then I'll have to sort out something with this marshal, but for the moment I simply want you away from Haze. We'll ride through the night; the sooner you, the money and your pa's claim are back where they should be, the better. Who knows what's happened since we've been gone. Your name's probably been added to Marshal Cridland's warrant by now.'

She reached out and held him. He could feel she was shaking. 'Saddle our three horses, Scrap,' he said to the boy, who seemed happy enough to leave the mine.

Leah looked back to the shaft; they

could hear Haze ranting and raving.

'We gotta go, Leah,' said Pope, his voice gentle. He knew from the enthusiasm with which she'd returned his embraces that she cared for him as much as he for her. She trusted him and would do what he asked. She nodded and they headed out to the sunlight.

They didn't get very far, though. Standing on the ledge outside the doorway was Jack Cannon, his six shooter pressed against Scrap's temple, while his sons grinned malevolently behind him. 'Now ain't this just peachy,' he sneered.

* * *

Jack's plan was simple. He would take Pope and Haze to Festival Ridge and claim the reward for the wanted men, then return Leah to her family.

'My wife,' he said, 'God rest her almost dead soul, won't last another summer, then I'll be looking for another woman. Reckon you'll be feeling pretty grateful to me, miss, for saving you from these outlaws. Then, ranching being the dangerous business it is, there's only an accident to happen to Shady, and the whole spread'll be mine. It's a dandy plan, now, you gotta admit it.'

Leah spat at him, Pope remained impassive and Haze began to warble like a demented Indian.

'What you got planned for me?' asked Scrap.

'You die,' said Cannon, pointing his gun at him, 'now, or later. Later, I'm having too much fun at the moment.'

With the help of his sons, Cannon had taken Pope's and Haze's weapons and tied their hands behind them. They had all negotiated the wooden walkway, and the Cannon family were now pushing them on to their horses.

'I can't leave,' shouted Haze, in between warbles. 'I've got to paint two more eyes. I gotta! I gotta paint your eyes, Jack. Oh yeah, once I've got your eyes up there, everything will be all right. I gotta paint the eyes.'

'Shut it!' screamed Cannon, blasting a bullet into the ground by Haze's feet. 'Reckon I'll shut you up for good before we get to town.'

'You'd better check whether the bounty's paid for dead or alive before you start destroying your assets,' said Pope quietly.

'Hell, I'm going to get the ranch and the woman; the bounty's just pin money,' snapped Cannon. 'Can't wait to see you hanging from the gallows though, Pope. Messing yourself, your eyes popping, your tongue lolling. Yeah, that's going to be a sight to treasure. And knowing that the last thing you'll be thinking, before Hell opens up to claim you, is that my hard cow-stained hands are going to be wandering all over your woman's body. And I ain't going to be gentle with her, I promise. How's that make you feel, big man?'

'Sick to my stomach, Jack,' said Pope truthfully.

'I'll kill myself before I'll let you touch me, Jack Cannon,' said Leah defiantly. 'Pa and Shady won't keep you on when I tell them what you've done.'

'No one listens to you, woman, ain't you figured that out yet?' said Cannon.

'Let's get them to town, Pa,' said his elder son. 'That lunatic's trilling's making my trigger finger awful itchy. Don't know how long I can last without plugging him.'

'Plug away, dear boy,' said Haze. 'Send me to Hell. I'll enjoy digging a nice deep fiery pit, ready just for you and your lovely kin.'

Pope sneaked a look at Scrap; he could see the boy was trembling with terror, yet keeping a brave expression on his face. 'Keep it up, kid,' whispered Pope. 'None of us are dead yet.' He'd probably die trying, but Pope had one main objective now, he had to save Leah and the boy, no matter what the cost.

9

The last time he'd been in the jail at Festival Ridge Pope hadn't noticed its filth and how much it stank. Now, with Leah in the adjoining cell, he was acutely aware of how disgusting it was.

The townsfolk had hastily appointed a temporary sheriff after Lionel's death, but he was a fresh-faced kid, plucked from the mayor's office. Confronted by the snarling, heavily armed Cannons, he had decided it was best to leave any decisions to Marshal Cridland, who was expected shortly. The only thing that bothered him was locking Leah in the same cell as the men, which he seemed to think was tantamount to turning the sheriff's office into a house of ill repute. So she was pushed into a cell on her own.

'How'd Lionel die?' Pope asked the new incumbent.

The young sheriff looked at him suspiciously.

'I'm asking because I don't know how he died, as I didn't kill him,' said Pope.

'Yeah,' said the new sheriff. 'How come it's your name on the warrant the marshal's got, then?'

'I don't know. Indulge me, tell me how Lionel died.'

'I need to know, too,' said Haze, sniffing and wiping a tear from his eye, 'on account of the special friendship I shared with Lionel.'

The sheriff gave a look of even greater distaste to Haze than he had given to Pope. 'We all know you're a bad man, Mr Willerby, everyone says so.'

'Must be true then,' sniffed Haze, returning to the bench along the wall and lying on it.

'So Lionel never recovered from the blow to his head?' persisted Pope.

'Well surely he didn't, Mr Gunfighter, due to the lead slug you'd shot into it.'

'Ah,' said Pope. 'Tell me, how's the grieving widower, Mr Simpson?'

'Still running his saloon, and making a big profit tonight out of them Cannons.'

'If they pay,' said Pope. 'Maybe you should warn friend Simpson to get the money off them first.'

'Oh, no, I ain't leaving this jail, mister.'

'I've no doubt that as soon as Mr Simpson hears that Haze is here, he'll be down anyway,' said Pope.

'Why?' asked the sheriff.

'On account of the fact Mr Willerby here killed his wife.'

The sheriff took a step back from the bars. 'Yeah?'

'Yeah,' said Haze's voice from the back of the cell. 'She was getting on my nerves. You're getting on my nerves, too, Sheriff. I do miss old Lionel. Many's the time I've sat at that table, shared a bottle of liquor and made eyes at the sheriff. Dear old Lionel. He couldn't resist me — '

'Shut it, Haze,' said Pope. 'The new sheriff don't like that kinda talk.' He looked into the corner of the cell, where Scrap sat as close as he could to the bars that separated them from Leah's cell. She, on her own side, sat as close to him as she could. Pope turned back to the sheriff. 'The woman and the kid shouldn't be here. Marshal Cridland ain't going to be too impressed with you incarcerating two civilians on the word of some ignorant, drunk cowhand. You let them go, now, you hear?'

The man shook his head.

'You've got no power to hold them. Let them go and I'll confess to the murder of Lionel, Stella Simpson, Abraham Lincoln and just about anyone else you care to name.'

'I'm not going anywhere without you, Simeon,' Leah said softly but firmly. 'But Nathaniel's got no place here.'

Scrap pushed himself further into the corner of the cell. 'This town's full of Cannons. I'm staying here.'

Suddenly Haze fell to the floor and

began writhing, holding his stomach and squealing with pain. Pope knelt down and crouched over him.

'I need my stuff,' gasped Haze, his complexion suddenly pallid and glazed with sweat. Pope nodded. 'Sheriff, this man needs medicine. Go to his saddle-bag, get me the glass bottle and the needle from there. The sort of needle a doctor uses, you know. Get it, now! He's dying.'

The lawman looked confused, but before he had time to move the door burst open and Simpson, armed with a rifle, stumbled inside.

'Where's the murdering bastard who killed my wife!' he shouted. 'Haze Willerby! Where is he?'

Haze groaned that he was already dying, and muttered something about wanting to be put out of his misery.

The sheriff pulled his gun. 'Can't have you waving that rifle about in here, Mr Simpson,' he said. 'You put that weapon down and leave this to the judge, eh?'

'Well said, son,' said Pope approvingly.

'Hell to the judge, I want revenge!' screamed Simpson. 'I shot that pervert sheriff because he let the murderer of my wife walk free. Now God has brought Willerby back so I can kill him and get justice for Stella!'

Simpson took aim at the writhing Haze, but the sheriff stepped in front of him. 'I can't let you do that, sir. And since you've confessed, I'll have to arrest you for the murder of Sheriff Pike.'

Simpson's rifle waved around and spittle sprayed from his mouth as he screamed at the sheriff.

'I've no desire to kill you, boy,' he said, 'but if I have to, to get to Willerby, so be it.'

Pope stepped back from the front of the cell and indicated to Leah and Scrap that they should crouch down.

'Take this as a warning,' shouted Simpson, letting off a random shot, which reverberated like thunder around the confines of the jail. It was immediately followed by the sharp crack of pistol fire, and the saloon owner lay motionless on the ground.

'It was self-defence,' yelled the sheriff hysterically, throwing himself against the bars of the cell. 'You saw that, didn't you? I had no choice, it was him or me.' He began to sob.

It took no effort at all for Pope to relieve him of his weapon and pull it through the bars. He pointed it at the distraught man. 'At the very least, Sheriff, you oughta open up and put yourself in this cell. We'll leave it to the judge to decide if it was self-defence or not.'

The sheriff fell to his knees, crying hopelessly.

'The keys, son,' said Pope, 'or you're dead.' He cocked the pistol.

'Poor, poor man,' said Leah, rushing to the front of her cell, as the sheriff threw the keys across the floor. Scrap, who had also left the assumed safety of the rear of the cell, reached out and dragged them in. Within seconds Pope had released them all and Scrap had retrieved Haze's saddle-bag. Haze clutched it like it had saved his life and scuttled off.

'Cannon's going to kill me,' wailed the sheriff.

'You're right,' said Pope. 'Leah, you and the kid, make for the church. You go with them if you want, Sheriff. You should have a bit of safety there. I'll sort out Jack Cannon and his kin, once and for all. I should have done it long ago.'

Leah grabbed hold of him. 'No, Simeon, don't! That will be murder.'

Pope pushed her away. 'No, ma'am, it's extermination of vermin, which ain't murder at all.' He looked around; there was no sign of Haze, though he could guess what he was doing. 'And when you find Haze, take him to the church too.' Pope handed the sheriff's gun back to him. 'You were put in an impossible position, son. You did what you could.'

The sheriff ripped off his badge and threw it against the wall, then grabbed Leah's hand and dragged her out of the jail.

★   ★   ★

With disappointing predictability the Cannons were already causing trouble at Simpson's saloon. Liquor and bad language were flowing like a river in spate. Grappling and gunfire would follow as night follows day. Pope decided that he might as well be the one to start it. He pulled his pistol and fired up at the ceiling. There was a brief silence as plaster dust floated down like dirty snowflakes.

'It's him, Pa,' shouted the elder Cannon son. 'How'd he get out?'

Jack Cannon pushed himself, with unmerited violence, to the front of the crowd. 'I'd hoped to see you swing, Pope,' he said. 'But lead'll have to do.'

'Outside, Jack,' said Pope. 'This between you and me. Ain't no reason to involve anyone else.'

'What involves me, involves my boys,' said Cannon.

'That's three against one, that's not fair,' said a voice in the crowd. Cannon's younger son silenced the speaker with his fist.

'You want to die as a family, that's fine by me,' said Pope. 'Outside, all of you.' He backed slowly towards the saloon door.

A shot fired out. Jack Cannon dropped like a stone. Suddenly everyone was yelling and gun smoke filled the saloon. The crowd were no longer standing and staring but had become a mangled mêlée of writhing, fighting, firing bodies. Pope continued backing away, his eyes narrowed. He saw Cannon's younger son line up his pistol for a point-blank shot at a hapless bystander. Pope's shot didn't just take off his hat: half his skull blasted over the bar too.

There was a scream and the thunder of footsteps as Haze hurtled down from the balcony. His rifle held aloft in one hand, he was firing indiscriminately with the pistol he held in the other. He was yelling nonsense, shrieking like a banshee.

Pope shot into the air again. 'Stop!' he yelled, his voice carrying enough authority for everyone to cease what they were doing for a short moment. 'Stop now!' ordered Pope. 'Look around, who you all fighting? Each other, that's all. Can you see Cannon's other son, Haze?'

Haze swivelled around, then shook his head. 'The one still in possession of a full head of hair? No. Looks like the yellow belly ran off when daddy died.'

'Looks like he did.' Pope addressed the crowd. 'Who'd Simpson leave in charge when he went to the jailhouse?'

The barkeep, looking worried and wringing his hands in his apron, stepped tentatively forward. 'I generally tend things when the boss ain't here, sir,' he stuttered.

'Then you continue to generally tend

things, mister, since Simpson's dead, lying in the jail. Your sheriff shot him in self-defence; there's four witnesses to that.' Pope touched the brim of his hat, nodded to the stunned drinkers and left the saloon, Haze puffing behind him. 'Guess it was you shot Jack Cannon,' Pope said, lighting a cigarillo and not looking behind him. His eyes scanned the town, intent upon noticing any detail. Cannon's son's horse had gone, but that didn't mean he wasn't still around, ready to take a pot shot.

'Yep,' said Haze.

'I suppose I should thank you, between him and his boys one of them was sure to get me.'

'You're pretty quick and deadly accurate: my money would've been on you. Anyway I didn't kill Cannon for you.'

'Don't tell me he was getting on your nerves,' said Pope with a grim smile.

'He surely was, friend Popey, Pope.'

★ ★ ★

Relief spread over Leah's features when they entered the church, and she ran towards them. 'We heard gunfire but the sheriff wouldn't let me out,' she said.

'Quite right,' said Pope. 'Jack Cannon's dead, as is his younger son. The older one seems to have lost his nerve and run away, but we should keep vigilant.' He turned to the sheriff. 'I explained what happened with Simpson. This town's going to need a bit of help pulling itself together. I reckon you've the potential to show some leadership; you go and sort things out.'

'Me?' exclaimed the young sheriff, disbelievingly.

'Yes, you; but remember, keep an eye open in the back of your head for young Cannon.'

The sheriff nodded to Leah and left them.

'Time we headed back to your ranch, Leah,' said Pope. 'You need to sort out your family.' He sighed. 'At least we know Jack Cannon ain't going to be there.'

'Even though he was such a bad man I wish you hadn't had to kill him.'

'I didn't,' said Pope.

As half the population of Festival Ridge were congregated around the jailhouse and the other half were in the saloon, Pope helped himself to supplies from the unmanned general store, and left some money on the counter. By the time he'd done that Scrap and Haze had the horses ready and they and Leah were already mounted.

'Let's get you home,' said Pope to Haze and his sister, and the four of them galloped out of town.

* * *

Pope was satisfied with the progress they had made by the time they stopped that night. Their rations eaten, and with Scrap and Leah already wrapped in their blankets and asleep, Pope uncorked his whiskey and poured a good measure for himself and Haze into their empty coffee cups.

'Until I know exactly what happened to Junior Cannon I can't rest completely easy,' said Pope. 'So I reckon we should take it in turns to keep watch.'

'I don't sleep, remember,' said Haze. 'You get some shut-eye, Pope.'

'Maybe, in a minute,' said Pope, twisting his cup and looking at the contents rather than drinking from it. 'What you going to do, Haze?'

'Keep watch, I told you.'

'No, what you going to do when Marshal Cridland catches up with us, which he surely will?'

'I didn't kill Lionel. You heard Simpson. The sheriff at Festival Ridge and you can testify as to what happened there. I can't see the marshal's going to have any interest in me or you once he knows that.'

'And what about Stella?'

'From what you said that don't figure on the warrant.'

Pope sighed.

Haze leaned forward. 'Look here, Simeon Pope, I hardly know you at all, but I reckon you've killed a darn sight more folk than I have, so don't get judgemental, eh?'

'I wasn't,' said Pope. 'And, not that it's any of your business, I only use my gun when I have to.'

Haze sniggered and poured himself another drink. 'This is the Wild West, dear Popey, a man's best friend is his gun, but I'm happy to believe you ain't completely trigger happy. Though I wouldn't want your life, if this is what it's always like. Far too messy.'

Pope at last took a sip of whiskey. 'No, my life ain't usually like this. It only got messy when I got mixed up with you.'

'And you got greedy,' sneered Haze. 'Hired by Shady to kill me and by Pa to bring me home alive. How were you ever going square that?'

'Easy. You're dying, ain't you? All I had to do was ask Shady to be patient.'

'Go to sleep, Pope, you're getting on

my nerves now.'

Pope grunted, finished his drink, lay down and drew his blanket up to his chin.

★　★　★

Dawn had not quite broken when Pope awoke. Haze was sitting next to him; apart from the frantic tapping of his foot he was still, and wide awake.

Pope pulled himself to a sitting position. 'You really don't sleep?' he said softly, not wanting to disturb Leah or Scrap.

'You snore,' said Haze by way of reply, though he was smiling. 'Shall we wake our companions? We might as well make an early start.'

'Yeah, in a minute, we might as well,' said Pope. He and Haze sat in silence for a while, then Pope's body stiffened and he leaned closer to Haze. 'We ain't alone,' he whispered.

'You sure?' said Haze.

'Sure,' said Pope.

10

'Just keep talking nice and soft,' said Pope, nice and softly to Haze. 'Two tired men, murmuring together, you know what I mean?'

'Sure,' said Haze blandly. 'You really heard something, partner?'

'Yup. Hardly a breath but I heard something.'

'You reckon it's the last of the Cannon boys?' Haze was good, his voice showed hardly any expression and his words were only just discernible by Pope.

'Could be Cannon. Could be the marshal. Hell, Haze, we ain't been attacked by renegade Indians yet. I'm discounting nothing.' He raised his hands into the air and made a loud yawn. 'Reckon I'll just stretch my legs and go to that scrub yonder.'

'I see,' said Haze, likewise yawning

and getting up. 'You make sure you got your gun now, friend. Never know when you're going to disturb a rattler in these parts.'

'Sure will. If you venture away from the fire you should take your own advice.' Haze surreptitiously pointed a short distance away from where Pope was headed, and the two men left their places by the fire.

Pope cocked his weapon, and Haze did likewise.

'Got you covered both ways,' said Pope loudly. 'If I don't get you, my friend here will. Come out, show yourself.'

There was a rustling in the shrubs and Cannon's son walked out, his hands held high. 'Can't fool you, eh, Pope?' he said, and even in the dim light Pope could see the arrogant sneer curling his lips. It was not the expression of a defeated man. Something was wrong, Pope swivelled round just in time to hear Leah gasp and to see two other men pull her and Scrap from their beds and hold pistols to them.

'Drop your guns,' said Cannon, with a triumphant laugh catching his throat. 'See, boys, I told you Pope was stupid, and as for Haze Willerby, you won't find a madder man this side of the asylum wall.'

Haze threw down his gun. 'You're right, kid. I'm mad. Mad enough to rip you apart, which I will do at the first opportunity I get.'

Pope merely let his weapon slide to the ground. He had been stupid, but he could never have guessed that Cannon would join up with the other two men, whom he instantly recognized.

'Junior!' exclaimed Leah. 'What do you think you're doing? Let us go immediately!'

Junior Cannon picked up the guns, touched the brim of his hat and nodded to Leah. 'Now that's mighty big talk from a little lady, and I sure am sorry I'm gonna turn your brother in to the marshal, but he did kill my daddy in cold blood. I saw him do it with my own eyes, as did my new friends Santos and Theo. You were in the saloon, weren't you?'

Junior's two companions snarled.

'Yeah, we saw it. Just like we saw that man Pope kill our friend,' said Santos. 'Seeing you hang, Pope, and getting paid to hand you in is going to feel mighty sweet.'

Theo nodded, the corners of his mouth turned down, as if he was close to tears. ''Cos of you we've been forced into driftin'. It ain't been easy, Pope. Do you know what it's like to be hungry? It's been hard for us when we've been used to having our own spread.'

'Spread? Who're you kidding, Theo?' said Pope. 'You were trespassing on Mr Baxter's land; you weren't even making any attempt to work it. Not to mention rustling his cattle and causing all sorts of trouble whenever you could. Baxter had every right you see you off, and to hire me to make sure you left. I gave you boys every opportunity to leave peaceably. Grecko chose to fight and he lost. That was his decision.'

'He couldn't leave that land, not with his pa being buried there and all,' Theo said piously.

Santos snorted. 'Maybe he was, maybe he wasn't. All I know is Baxter had plenty of land and we got none.'

'Quit chawing about what's gone before,' snapped Junior. 'We all got reason to hate Pope. Bind up the prisoners and get them on to their horses. Last I heard Marshal Cridland was at Indian Tombs, so we head out that way. The sooner we catch up with the lawman the sooner we get our reward, and Pope and his loopy-loo friend hang.'

He turned to Leah. 'You've made a big mistake, Miss Willerby. You've always been kind to my ma, but stealing from your pa, now that ain't right, miss. You should have more respect. If I find your name's been added to that warrant, I'll be handing you in too.'

Junior paused as his none-too-quick brain chugged into action. 'You still got the money you took from old man Willerby?'

'No,' said Leah, acutely aware of the banknotes and Ham's claim held tight under her corsets, hoping none of their captors had the sense to search her.

'Where is it then?' wondered Junior, his forehead crazed with frown lines.

'I ate it!' chirped Haze, rolling his eyes as madly as only he could. 'I ate it, I ate it, I ate the money! And you know what happened then, sonny boy?'

Junior's eyes were wide, he shook his head dumbly.

'I felt sick!' Haze's manic cackle was only silenced by the back of Santos's hand slapping into his face.

'Looks like I've got to add you to my ripping apart list,' snarled Haze.

'At least let the child go, he's no use to you,' said Leah, but, knowing the answer, she did not wait for a reply. She turned to Theo, who was binding her wrists. 'Don't pull so tight, that hurts,' she snapped.

'Sorry, miss, sorry, sorry,' he muttered.

★ ★ ★

They were only a few miles outside Indian Tombs when they saw dust on the horizon.

'Well, if that's the marshal I hope he gives you all a good telling off for this. It's not right, you know, taking the law into your own hands.' Leah was the only one who had spoken much as they rode. Her tongue was sharp, and she wasn't afraid to lash out at her captors. Haze told her to keep quiet (she was getting on his nerves), but Pope was happy to let her keep talking. He could see that her words bothered Theo, and any edge that that gave him later he would be happy to exploit.

Within minutes Marshal Cridland and his posse surrounded them, guns drawn. Junior Cannon began mouthing off, but even he had the sense to show some respect to a US marshal accompanied by six armed and experienced men.

Leah was not so circumspect. 'Arrest these men now, Marshal,' she demanded. 'They jumped us in our camp and restrained us with ropes tied far too tightly. They are quite despicable men and deserve to be punished.'

'Now, now, Miss Willerby,' said the marshal, tiredly. 'I've heard you might be in no position to demand anything, seeing how you stole a deal of money and more from your pa. I'm minded to put you all into custody to stand trial. And I mean *all* of you.'

Junior and his gang made loud protests, but they were quickly disarmed by the marshal's men.

'It's too late to start for Festival Ridge,' said Cridland. 'I'm going to head back to the Willerby spread and keep you under detention there. Deputy Green, you go to the marshal's office and come back with a prison wagon and four more deputies. Ride as fast as you can, I don't want to keep these folks out of jail any longer than I have to.'

The deputy did as he was told, his horse disappearing in a cloud of dust.

'You can't put us in jail just like that,' exclaimed Leah. 'Whatever happened to the notion of being innocent until proven guilty?'

'Whatever happened to the notion of a woman knowing her place and keeping quiet?' said the marshal. 'One of the reasons I'm not making you ride through the night to Festival Ridge is on account of your being of the tender sex, miss. I was thinking you might appreciate the chance to freshen up at your own home.'

'Mighty grateful for that, I'm sure,' she muttered. 'And I don't suppose there's any point in me asking you to release the boy, who most surely is innocent.'

'No point at all, ma'am, no point at all,' said the marshal.

Cridland's men swiftly evicted the

remaining hands at the ranch from the bunkhouse and turned it into a temporary jail, incarcerating their male prisoners there. Taking Leah's word that she would not escape, Cridland allowed her back into the house.

Ham tearfully embraced her. 'What possessed you to do what you did, child?' he asked her sorrowfully.

'Madness,' she confessed. She tapped her side. 'It's all here, Pa, hidden in my underwear. I'm going to get changed and then you'll have your money and your claim back in your safe. Haze meant well, but Pa, I've got to warn you, he's not at all well.'

'Haze!' exclaimed Ham. 'Where is he?'

'Here, arrested with the rest of us. Sit down, Pa, pour us a drink and I'll explain what happened.'

★ ★ ★

In the bunkhouse Junior and his associates formed themselves into a snarling gaggle at one end of the room, while Pope, Haze and Scrap sat around a table at the other end. One of the deputies stood in the corner of the room, eyes alert, gun ready.

Pope and Haze were smoking and appeared relaxed, Scrap was more obviously anxious. 'I ain't keen on spending the night with them,' he said, shooting a quick look at the other end of the room. Junior stared at them and ran his hand across his neck in warning.

Pope shook his head dismissively. 'You'll be all right, kid. Even now I expect Leah's chewing the marshal's ear about you.'

'And boy, can she chew,' said Haze. 'What do you think, Pope? Should we escape, or just kill that trash over there?'

Pope let out a long stream of smoke from his lips. 'Dunno,' he replied honestly. 'I've no desire to stand trial, that's for sure. I don't think I've actually broken any laws, but a judge may not see it that way. I don't want to compound the trouble I'm in by adding escape and murder to Cridland's list of crimes, though.'

'I'm a murderer already, but I'll be dead before any judge gets to try me.' Haze sounded cheerful enough with his prognosis.

Pope dropped the butt of his cigarillo and ground it into the floor with his boot. 'And ill man that you are, you'll be needing your medicine soon.'

'I will,' said Haze. 'Sounds to me like you've got a plan, friend.'

'No,' said Pope. 'I've got hopes, but no plans. Not just yet anyway.'

★　★　★

Leah explained what had happened to her incredulous father, returned his property to him, and persuaded him not to further antagonize the marshal by demanding an immediate meeting with Haze. Leaving Ham alone to ponder over what had happened she proceeded to do exactly what Pope had predicted.

'And another thing, Marshal,' she continued. 'If anything were to happen to that poor child whilst in your custody, what would that do for your career? You'd be guilty of negligence at the very least. You'd find it hard even to get employment as a guard on the railroad after that. And what a loss to the world of law-keeping that would be. But if you remain stubborn-headed about this, that's just what'll happen to you.

'Of course a wise and sensible man would know what to do. You've got four hardened criminals and a madman holed up in our bunkhouse. The child isn't even fifteen. The potential for the corruption of that boy is immense. Leave him in there just one night and you could have created another criminal. Let him out under my care and come back in five years' time and you'll find as fine a US citizen as you could ask for.'

'And how are you going to do that, ma'am, when you're likely to be in prison yourself?' Cridland tried to reason.

'For what crime? My father has his money and his claim. Locked away in his safe. He'll show you if you like. He must have mislaid them. How can I be convicted for a crime that was never committed?'

Cridland let out a long sigh.

★ ★ ★

Pope looked at his watch. 'The marshal's ears will be bleeding by now, I reckon. Scrap, when you get out, go and find Haze's medicine and bring it to the guards here. Cridland ain't inhumane, and once Haze gets to writhing about we'll all want to do anything we can to put him right.'

Haze nodded enthusiastically. 'I'm starting to feel a bit jittery already.'

'Tell Leah to have a bag packed ready. If things kick off here, we may need to leave in a hurry. If she can find some way to get to speak to me, so much the better.'

Scrap was still looking doubtful when Cridland came into the room in the bunkhouse and called his name. Scrap spoke briefly to him, then, with a swift backward look to Pope and Haze he followed the marshal out.

Junior and his associates immediately began to complain, but Cridland's answer to that was to send in another armed guard.

Haze settled back into his chair and took some cards from his pocket. Pope nodded when offered a game.

'Any of you boys fancy being whopped at cards?' Haze called across the room. Theo looked like he might be interested, but the derisive answer of the other two forced him to ignore the offer.

11

Ham was getting impatient. It had been years since he'd seen Haze and he didn't understand why, when his son was as close as his own bunkhouse, he couldn't speak to him.

Now that she had secured Scrap's release Leah wasn't so bothered about upsetting the marshal, and she let her father berate him. She wished she had some sort of plan that would prevent Haze and Pope being carted back to Festival Ridge. She had sent one of the remaining hands to come back with the family attorney but, as he was based over fifty miles away, she was not hopeful that he would arrive before the prison wagon and the extra marshals. She was disappointed in Pope as well. The only message he had passed, via Scrap, was that she should have a bag packed and try to talk to him if she could. Cridland had the bunkhouse so tightly guarded she hadn't managed the latter, nor did she like the implication that Pope intended some sort of break-out. Much as she desired Pope, and would like to be with him, being an outlaw's woman didn't appeal. She looked at the meal she had made. Cridland would have to let the men eat, maybe that would give her a chance to contact Pope.

★　★　★

Ham was standing in the middle of the yard, one of Cridland's men had his rifle practically pushed up Ham's nose.

'Haze, son, I'm going to get you out,' screamed Ham. 'You, boy,' he stabbed his finger at the deputy, 'you get that no-good boss of yours out here, now! This is my ranch, I'm telling you, let my son go! I'm going to be writing to the governor about this.

Hell, I'm going to be writing to the president himself.'

The lawman stood, silent and implacable. The problem was, Leah thought, as she walked across the yard with the tray of food, that Cridland did actually have the law on his side. Haze was a self-confessed murderer, though his mental state should mitigate against any sentence he was given. As for Pope, he might technically not have broken any laws, but he was definitely no angel. How she wished Indian Tombs was large enough to support its own legal practice; she was sure a good lawyer would at least ensure that Haze could be released to a hospital.

'Leave it, Pa,' she said as she drew level with her father. 'Marshal Cridland,' she called loudly. 'I've some food here, for you, your men, and the prisoners.'

Cridland came out of the bunkhouse. 'I'll take some for the prisoners,' he said. 'My men will stick to their own rations.'

Leah raised her eyebrows. 'You think I'd try to poison you? How ridiculous!'

Cridland called for another of his men to take the tray and shrugged. 'Ma'am, I've learned to trust no one.' He turned to his deputy. 'Dole out this food to the prisoners, but check through it first. I don't want messages being passed.'

'You really are insulting me now, Marshal,' she snapped.

'I seen the way you and that Pope feller sneak adoring looks at each other. I don't trust you for one single solitary moment, ma'am, begging your pardon if that causes offence. As for you, Mr Willerby, you got a big spread to run. I suggest you get on with your business and leave me to get on with mine.'

'I shall be reporting you to your superiors, I assure you,' shouted Ham at Cridland's back. He turned to Leah. 'I'm going to ride out and get Shady, he'll sort this out.'

Leah said nothing. She was pleased

to have her father out of the way for a while.

★ ★ ★

It was hot in the bunkhouse. Cridland had ordered the shutters to be closed once Ham had started screaming from outside. The stale, sticky air was doing nothing to improve the tempers of the prisoners.

'We're all cursed,' said Haze in his smoothly unhinged but compelling way. 'Indian Tombs: that says it all, doesn't it?'

'Shut ya blotchy face, you madman,' shouted Junior. 'Ignore him!' he ordered his companions.

'That was what was here when the first settlers arrived. Tombs.' Haze lowered his voice and it boomed sepuchrally across the room. 'Indian Tombs. The long-dead braves of the past, bound into their war clothes, lying on raised beds, so the crows and the vultures could pick off their flesh, bit by

174

bit, peck by delicious meaty peck.' He licked his lips. 'What wasn't taken by the birds, was sucked off by the maggots, till the bones were left white. Gleaming white in the sunlight, and the souls of the Indian braves were quiet and free to commune with the Great Spirit. And then what?'

Haze paused briefly. 'Then the first settlers came, and they pulled down those sacred resting places of the Indians, stopped them braves looking skywards and threw away their bones.' Haze jumped up and stamped his feet. 'This is hallowed ground, and you don't mess with hallowed ground.'

Pope also stood up, moved to the wall and pressed his back against it.

'Cursed, cursed, everyone last damned one of us. And we deserve it, for what our forefathers did,' Haze continued.

The deputy in the corner shook his rifle. 'Shut it, Willerby,' he ordered.

'What you going to do, shoot me? We're all going to die.' He turned back to Junior and his companions. 'And then what? Then we'll see the skeletons of the long-dead braves coming for us, their white teeth gnashing, ready to tear our flesh from us, rip, rip, rip. For ever and ever, eternally for ever, rip, rip, rip. Exquisite, unimaginable pain.'

Theo was crying as loudly as a newborn, Santos also didn't look that confident, but Junior hurled himself towards Haze, only stopping when a bullet sent up splinters of wood from the bunkhouse floor in front of him. His big face was puce as he screamed at the lawman. 'You can't kill me, I'm unarmed!'

'It's OK, Marshal, just a warning,' the deputy shouted through the door, before turning back to Junior. 'It's my duty to keep order in this bunkhouse, I think you'll find the law is on my side, boy, no matter what I do.'

'You don't have to worry about the law,' said Haze, his voice superbly sinister. 'What we all gotta worry about is justice. The justice and punishment we all face for desecrating hallowed ground.'

Everyone stopped and stared as the door opened and Cridland and a deputy came in, carrying the food.

'Chow time,' said Cridland. 'Come and get a bowl, orderly like.' He looked around the room. Theo had squashed himself, face down, into a corner, his whole body racked with sobs. Santos had rallied a little and forced a smug smile on his face, though it looked as if it was about to slip off at any time. The red-faced Junior stood in a threatening pose.

'What the hell's been going on?' asked Cridland.

'Some daft storytelling from the madman's got everyone jittery,' said the deputy.

Cridland blew out a dismissive jet of air from his mouth. 'Keep quiet and eat up,' he ordered as the tray was placed on to the table.

Haze skipped over and spat into every bowl but one, which he handed to

Pope. 'Come and catch some madness from me, boys,' he chortled. Cridland caught hold of him.

'Right, Willerby, I'm putting you in solitary,' he said, guiding Haze towards the door.

'Thanks, friend, that leaves three against one,' muttered Pope, quickly taking some mouthfuls of food.

'I'll make sure you get a fair trial, Pope, or die in the attempt,' said Cridland as he grappled with an increasingly agitated Haze.

'Looks like that's the likely way it's going to end,' said Pope.

Haze kicked and spat and lunged at Cridland's neck, sinking his teeth into the flesh. The deputy pulled him off, Cridland staggered back unbelievingly, grasping his wound.

Haze disentangled himself from the deputy and writhed on the floor, his red-rimmed mouth shooting spittle, his dreadful, bone-rattling cough echoing sickly about the room.

'He's ill, dying, he needs medicine.

Scrap, the boy, he knows where it is,' said Pope. He could hear banging on the door and Leah's voice. 'Get away, Leah!' he shouted. 'Far away, keep away!'

Haze was shrieking now, Theo had turned round and was trying to push himself as far into the corner as he could, his feet kicking and slipping against the floorboards, his fearful howling matching Haze's in intensity. Santos was shouting something, and Junior hurled himself towards the deputy, who was staring, both compelled and horrified, at Haze. Junior easily wrested his gun from him and held him in front as a shield.

'Kill me, kill me! I deserve punishment, I wanna die, kill me!' screamed Theo, and Junior couldn't help himself but oblige, his shot splattering the poor boy's bowels over the bunkhouse wall. That gave the deputy time to pull away and to allow his colleague to plug Junior with his rifle, the force of the bullet sending him into the air before he landed on the ground in an untidy heap.

Santos stopped shouting and stood stock still, his hands held so high his shoulders were in danger of dislocating. Pope stood impassively, his back to the wall, while Haze continued writhing.

Cridland struggled to pull himself upright. 'Situation under control,' he called as his remaining deputies ran into the room, guns ready. 'Bring the boy with Willerby's medicine,' he ordered breathlessly, and Pope at last moved from his position, to place a chair behind the marshal, who gratefully fell into it.

'I ain't going to hurt you,' said Pope, looking at Cridland's wound. 'And this ain't going to kill you,' he assured the lawman, 'but you might want to get Miss Willerby to tend to it.' He let his finger run down his own cheek. 'She fixed me up pretty well.'

Cridland dabbed his neckerchief on the wound. 'I'll sort myself out,' he gasped.

A deputy returned with Haze's bag, and soon, his opium delivered, the raving man was replaced by a heavy-lidded and placid individual. 'Two to one, now.' He winked at Pope, as the bodies of Junior and Theo were dragged out of the bunkhouse.

'Plus a marshal and five deputies,' said Pope as he gently lifted Haze on to a chair.

Haze nuzzled into him. 'You're such a comfort to me, Popey,' he said with a yawn.

★　★　★

Ham and Shady were riding into the yard as the deputies were pulling the bodies from the bunkhouse.

'That's it, I'm getting Haze outta there before he comes to any harm. You sure he's all right, girl?' said Ham to Leah, who had rushed to meet them.

'The marshal assures me he's fine now he's had his medicine.'

Ham spurred his horse to the bunkhouse.

Shady glowered down at her from his mount. 'Pity.' He spat the word under his breath.

She looked up at him. 'Please, Shady, he's your brother, and he's not well. Can't you find it in yourself to forgive him?'

'Nope, sister,' he said, slipping down from his horse. 'I can't find it in my heart to forgive him for what he's done to Pa.'

It was true: for years after he left, Ham had mourned his elder son as if he were dead. Shady had had to learn quickly how to run the ranch.

'Haze is dying, Shady,' she said.

Her brother leaned towards her. 'Haven't you noticed how much better Pa's been recently? Haze being here and dying all over again ain't going to do Pa, me, you or the ranch any good, is it? Haze should have stayed away, and you shouldn't have encouraged him to come back. It's a pity that gun-slinger boyfriend of yours is under arrest; you could have ridden off with him, 'cause you sure ain't welcome here no more.'

Leah blinked back tears. 'Shady, do you hate me so much?'

He looked at her with disdain. 'I don't hate you, sister. You're just stupid, stupid like Pa. Blind to everything but Haze's charm. I've been working my butt off for seven years, keeping you and Pa. Keeping this ranch going. And what thanks do I get? The both of you writing to that waster behind my back. Not a word of thanks, or appreciation, just betrayal. I need Pa, I need to inherit the ranch from him, but I don't need you, sister. I don't need to eat your fancy food, and if the house gets dirty, so who cares.' He stomped away, leaving her with his horse.

She stroked the pinto's nose. 'Hell of a mess, boy,' she said. 'One hell of a mess.'

* * *

Despite his earlier protestations Make-peace Cridland did ask Leah to examine his wound, though by the time he got to her it had stopped bleeding, and all she had to do was wash it and wrap some clean linen around it.

'I'm sorry,' she said. 'Haze is mad. I'm not sure he knows what he's doing, or why. I know the doctor at Festival Ridge wanted him to go to hospital. Can't you recommend that, Marshal? It can't be right for a sick man like Haze to go to prison.'

Cridland shrugged. 'That ain't up to me, ma'am. I gotta follow the law. I gotta treat everyone the same.'

'And I really don't think Pope has committed any crime,' said Leah, refusing to listen to what Cridland said.

'You can keep trying, Miss Willerby, but my answer's always going to be the same.'

She sighed. 'At least let my father see Haze. Even prisoners are allowed visitors, aren't they? Pa's been standing outside two hours now, he'll go mad too, if we leave him like that. Then he'll start shooting and then your deputies will kill him. Please let him see his son. And if you'd let me see Pope, I'd be mighty grateful too.'

Cridland leaned back in his chair and drained the coffee Leah had made for him. 'I'll trouble you for another cup, ma'am,' he said. 'That's mighty fine compared to lawman's rations.'

Leah obliged and gave him a slice of cake.

'You're thinking to win me over with cake and coffee, ma'am?'

'No, I'm hoping to appeal to your sense of honour and decency.'

'Very well. I'll bring Haze and Pope into the yard. They will both be handcuffed to a deputy, and with another deputy on guard, as well as myself in attendance. You can have ten minutes. That should be plenty of time. You happy now, Miss Willerby?'

'Thank you, Marshal Cridland, I am content.'

12

Haze came out first. He was calm and didn't seem bothered either that he was handcuffed to a lawman, or that he was meeting his father for the first time for years.

Ham didn't even try to hide his emotions but burst into tears and ran towards his son, pulling him tightly to him, despite Haze's and the marshal's protestations that he should not. Cridland watched closely and kept his gun at the ready.

'Quit clawing at me, old man,' said Haze, trying to push away his father, who just kept squeezing him tighter.

Leah stood outside the ranch house with Shady. She could feel the anger bubbling inside her brother with volcanic intensity. She tried to reach out to him, but he stepped away.

'My son, my son,' blubbed Ham, into

Haze's ear. 'I'll get you out of this, I promise, my son.'

'Now you're saying something I want to hear,' whispered Haze, rewarding his father with a kiss on the cheek. 'And make it soon. I've no desire to be dragged back to Festival Ridge in the marshal's wagon. Hell, Pa, I've no desire to go to prison either. Nor has Pope.'

'I ain't bothered about him, son,' replied Ham, still holding Haze close. 'And when I've got this bit of bother sorted out, then I'm gonna get you the best doctor ever. You'll be cured, son, and you'll be home for ever.'

'Hmm,' said Haze. 'Just spring me and Pope first, eh?'

Pope came out, likewise chained to a deputy. Leah went to him. 'I've sent for our lawyer. Even if you do have to stand trial you won't be convicted.'

'Yeah, well, that's appreciated,' said Pope, though he didn't sound convinced.

Leah felt awkward. 'You're not hurt

or anything, are you?'

'No, ma'am.'

This was hopeless. Whatever Pope wanted to say to her and she to him, it couldn't be uttered while he was tied to a lawman.

'What happened to Theo and Junior?'

'Junior snatched a gun from the deputy, shot Theo and got killed for it. Fair enough.'

'Theo was just a frightened boy.'

'That's true, ma'am, but Junior got what was coming to him.'

Leah looked away. She had started to cry and felt helpless and useless. 'I'm sorry, Pope,' she said, not turning to look at him.

'Yeah,' said Pope. 'Nothing's panned out the way I'd hoped.'

She swallowed hard. 'No, nothing,' she breathed. She looked to her father. Ham had disentangled himself from Haze.

'He's thirsty, I'm getting him some water,' he called to the marshal, and headed towards the butt.

Pope felt anxious, Leah looked at him, and he could see she was uneasy too. 'Reckon we've concluded our business, ma'am,' he said with a nod of his head. 'You take yourself off, now.'

She stayed where she was.

'Marshal Cridland,' called Ham from the water butt, 'if this isn't the darndest thing.' He waved the lawman over.

Cridland was no fool, and keeping his eye on the prisoners, he made his way slowly to Ham. 'Willerby, whatever you're up to I suggest you reconsider. You start messing with the law, you'll lose, trust me.'

'No, you lose,' said Ham, and with a swiftness which defied his years, he snatched a gun from behind the butt and rammed the barrel into Cridland's temple, while his left hand grasped Cridland's right so hard the lawman was forced to drop his own gun. Ham kicked it well away. 'Steady, boys,' said Ham to the deputies. 'Nice and steady now, hand your guns over to Haze and Pope, then unlock the cuffs.'

189

'Don't!' ordered Cridland.

Ham pressed his gun further into the marshal's temple and cocked it. 'You wanna see what the marshal's brains look like, that's fine by me.'

Shady ran over. 'Pa, you damned fool!' he cried.

The two deputies had no wish to see their boss killed; they handed over their weapons and unlocked the cuffs. Pope immediately pulled his deputy in front of him, pressing the gun into his back. Haze let go of his and the lawman ran back into the bunkhouse.

'Stand-off,' Leah heard Pope mutter under his breath.

'You'll lose, you know that,' said the deputy he held at gunpoint.

'Nathaniel!' shouted Leah, seeing the boy peeping out from the bunkhouse door.

'Stay there, kid,' ordered Pope.

Haze was strutting around the yard. 'I'm free! I'm free!' he declared.

Shady stepped forward. 'You're mad. No you're not, you're evil, Haze.

Everything you touch turns rotten and you gotta be stopped.' He pulled his gun.

Haze likewise aimed his weapon at Shady, though he could not hold it steady.

'No, no, no,' screamed Ham, pushing Cridland to the ground and rushing between his sons. 'No!' he screamed as Shady's bullet got him and spun him round, allowing Haze's slug to slam into Shady's chest. Haze was screaming with laughter now as he leapt and danced around.

'Get clear,' ordered Pope. He pushed the deputy he was holding away from him. The man wasn't quick enough and Haze got the lawman in the shoulder. Then Haze turned and looked at Pope. 'Time to say goodbye, Popey,' he said.

Pope threw his gun across the yard. 'You gotta stop this killing, Haze. Looks like you've done for your brother, and probably your pa too. Why? What for? What have you gained? And don't say they were getting on your nerves, 'cause that just ain't reason enough to kill.'

Haze pursed his lips petulantly. 'You're getting really disappointing now, Pope. I'm beginning to think you're nothing but talk. You're no big gun-slinger at all, just some well-dressed confidence trickster with an expensive gun and sparkly eyes.'

'I ain't got a gun, Haze, expensive or not. Kill me and you'll be committing cold-blooded murder, and in front of a US marshal. Even Leah's attorney won't be able to get you off that charge.'

Haze cackled demonically. 'I don't care. I'm as good as dead anyway. Doesn't anyone ever listen to what I'm saying?' He paused and kicked the ground. 'But you're right, Pope, I won't shoot you down like a dog. Pick up the weapon and we'll draw, shall we?'

'No,' said Pope. 'Then I would be putting you down like a dog. Give up, Haze, and we'll try and get you some treatment.'

'Only one treatment will cure me,' muttered Haze. Then he pulled himself upright from his shambling stance and pointed his gun, steady, with no hint of shaking, at Leah. 'I'm going to count to five, Pope. You get a gun and face me, or Leah gets it.'

Hot, acid rage burned up through Pope's body, searing every nerve. Five seconds gave him no chance of reaching the gun he'd so thoughtlessly tossed away.

'One, two.'

Pope heard a 'psst' behind him. Swiftly he sneaked a look. It was Scrap, standing in the bunkhouse door. In a split second he threw Pope's six-shooter to him. It arched through the air and landed snugly in the palm of his hand. 'Face me!' Pope screamed at Haze.

Leah heard a scream and realized it was herself. A shot fired, its loudness echoing in her ears. For a while everything was black. Then she opened her eyes and saw Haze flat on his back on the ground. Pope was running over to him.

Leah joined Pope seconds later.

'Shady's dead. Pa's injured, but Marshal Cridland was right there and stopped the bleeding, I don't reckon it will kill him.'

'Ah,' said Haze.

She looked down at him, amazed. 'You're still alive!' she exclaimed, tears brimming out of her eyes.

'At the moment, sis, but I ain't much longer for this world.' He looked up at Pope. 'Thank you, friend,' he said, reaching out and clutching Pope's hand. 'I knew you'd be the one to save me. Thank you.'

'Reckon I've killed you,' said Pope. 'You didn't give me time to aim properly, but you deserve it, you bastard, using your sister like that.'

'Thank you,' said Haze again. He looked peaceful, his blotchy complexion was suddenly smooth and clear. 'I gotta confess,' he said.

'Hell, Haze, I ain't no priest,' said Pope.

'I don't need a priest, I'll be pleading my case before the Almighty himself in a short while. Get me that idiot Cridland. He needs to know who did what, and that you did nothing, Popey.'

Cridland was soon beside them. Leah cradled Haze's head in her lap, and he still held on to Pope's hand. 'You got a notebook, Makepeace?' croaked Haze. 'I'm failing fast. I'm a dying man, soon to meet his maker, you trust I'm going to tell you the truth?'

'For once, sir, I do,' said the marshal, licking the tip of his pencil.

★   ★   ★

After the gunfight everything had been hectic. Pope and Cridland had got Ham to his room and Leah had dressed his wounds. The dead were buried and Cridland spent some time writing a lengthy report. By dusk the prison wagon arrived, though the only prisoner was a distressed Santos, who proclaimed loudly, and it seemed genuinely, that his only desire now was to lead a quiet honest life, should he be allowed to do so, and as far away from Indian Tombs as possible. Although he could be charged with the kidnap of Leah and her companions, the fact that neither she nor Pope wanted to press any charges probably meant he would do just that.

Leah had fed the marshal and his men and then spent a long time with her father. It was after midnight when she left his room and Pope was waiting for her.

'You got that bag packed?' he asked.

Her eyes shone as she looked at him. 'Doesn't matter, I can't leave now.'

He reached out to her but she stepped away from him. 'Why not?'

'Why not? Isn't it obvious? Not only has my father been injured, but he's lost both his sons. I can't leave him now.'

'I'm sorry about that. They were your brothers as well as his sons and I know you're grieving, but Ham will get better. Then what will you do?'

'There's the ranch to run.'

'And you're going to do that?'

'Sure.' She paused and swallowed hard. 'There's no point me telling you how I feel about you, Simeon. It'll just make things harder for both of us, but if I left with you now I couldn't be happy. I have to stay.'

Pope sucked in his angry breath. 'Why do you put him, your father, who has never bothered with you, before me, knowing how I care for you and will give you nothing but love and affection?'

'I'm staying because it's the right thing to do. It's the only thing I can do.' She walked away from him and he didn't either follow her or try to stop her.

★   ★   ★

Cridland and his men left early the next morning. After a breakfast with Leah spent in silence, Pope decided it was time to leave. He stood on the porch, buckled his gunbelt around his waist, and slipped his pistol into the holster.

He pulled his jacket straight and everything felt comfortable at last. Except for the hole he felt growing in his heart and which he was doing his best to ignore. He saw the boy in the yard and went over to him.

'You want to ride into town with me, Scrap? Reckon I owe you a drink and a steak at the very least.'

Scrap shook his head. 'No, sir. Miss Willerby's offered me a job here. I'm going to be a real cowboy.'

Pope's smile was genuine and he held out his hand. 'That's good to hear, boy. It's a fine opportunity; you make sure you make the best of it, now.'

'I fully intend to, sir. And Miss Willerby says that when everything's calmed down and her pa's feeling better, she's going to teach me reading, writing all the letters, numbers and everything.'

'Good. I've a lot to thank you for, Scrap, and it pleases me I'm leaving you in a better situation than I found you.'

'Leaving? You mean you ain't just going into town to get your stuff?'

'Getting my stuff and moving on.'

Scrap's eyes were wide. 'Moving on? Where to?'

'Same place I always go. The next place.'

'But Miss Willerby,' said Scrap softly.

'She won't come with me,' said Pope, equally softly.

'I suppose Miss Willerby don't want to go to the next place,' mused the boy.

'Oh, she made that very clear to me, son.'

Scrap sighed. 'Why do *you* have to go to the next place, when everything you want is here?'

Pope stopped and stood stock still in the middle of the yard.

'Do you want me to go and saddle Baxter?' he heard Scrap say, as if he was a million miles away; then he turned on his tail and ran back to the ranch house.

Leah was in the kitchen washing up the breakfast plates.

'I hear you've offered that kid, Scrap, that son of the saloon, a job!' exclaimed Pope breathlessly.

She turned from the sink and wiped her hands. 'That kid, who's saved your life on a couple of occasions, shows potential.'

'And you've offered to teach him reading and writing. Yet you've offered me nothing!'

'I assumed you were perfectly literate.'

'Damn you, Leah,' he said, rushing over and grasping her shoulders. 'You never offered me a job. You never asked me to stay.'

'I didn't feel I could. You've always made it clear you were moving on.'

She was right. 'That's because I've never really thought about it. I suppose I've never had an alternative. Would you like me to stay, Leah?'

She nodded. 'Of course,' she said, her voice cracking.

He picked her up and swung her around. 'And for the sake of decency, we'll have to get married, you agree?'

'Oh yes, Simeon.' She wrapped her arms tightly around him.

'Hell, we might as well adopt that kid Scrap while we're at it!'

'Nathaniel,' she corrected him.

He kissed her softly, then stood back, smiling broadly. 'Simeon Pope, from gunfighter to family man in less than a minute,' he said proudly. It already felt good.

Epilogue

The Willerbys lawyers had sent one of their junior partners, Felix Holloway. But by the time he arrived there was nothing for him to do, save help Ham change his will. Not that the partner minded his almost wasted journey at all, for it turned out that he knew Pope and was happy to spend time with an old family friend. He was also pleased to accept Leah's invitation to stay overnight at the ranch.

The evening meal finished, Pope and Ham played chess, while Scrap looked on intently. Leah took her coffee out on to the porch.

'Do you mind if I smoke, ma'am?' asked Felix, as he joined her.

'No, not at all,' she replied. 'Do you plan on an early start tomorrow?'

'I'd better,' he said, the flame of his match illuminating his face in the twilight. 'I'll be sorry to go. It's been a long time since I've seen Pope, it's been good to be with him. And good to see him so settled.'

'Hmm,' said Leah, putting down her coffee cup. 'I'm still not sure I understand the exact nature of your relationship with Simeon, though.'

Felix shrugged. 'I guess that's because I don't either. He and my mother go way back, that's all I know. What I've never been told, but what I strongly suspect, is that Pope not only set up Ma with the dress shop, he saw me and my brother through college too.'

Leah took a deep breath. 'I have to ask this; is he your father?'

Felix laughed. 'Why, no, ma'am! My mother's older than Pope, and I just about remember my pa. He must have died when I was about five.'

Leah sighed. 'I see. Or rather I don't see at all. I presumed Simeon had been so good to your family because of a . . . connection, um . . . special fond-ness for your mother.'

'Oh he's specially fond of Ma, all right, but as far as I know it's never progressed beyond the parlour into another room, if you catch my drift.'

Leah nodded.

'And I know no one will be happier than my ma when she hears that Pope has found someone at last. You must visit her, you'll get on. Pope may have bought the shop in the first place, but she's put in all the hard work to make it the success that it is. There's not a society bride in Denver doesn't walk down the aisle in a Ellen Holloway gown.'

Leah smiled. 'Well, I shall be wearing my Sunday-best dress when I marry Simeon, but yes, I hope I shall meet her, and soon.' She paused. 'It's strange, but I don't feel at all unsure of marrying a man who I know has something of a suspect past, and many secrets.'

'I think I know what you mean, ma'am. I know my family is successful because of gunfighting money, but because it comes from Pope I'm not ashamed of that. I suppose it's because the man's got integrity.'

'Yes,' said Leah softly. But patiently, little by little, she would find out the true story of Simeon Pope.

THE END

We do hope that you have enjoyed reading this large print book.

Did you know that all of our titles are available for purchase?

We publish a wide range of high quality large print books including:
Romances, Mysteries, Classics
General Fiction
Non Fiction and Westerns

Special interest titles available in large print are:
The Little Oxford Dictionary
Music Book, Song Book
Hymn Book, Service Book

Also available from us courtesy of Oxford University Press:
Young Readers' Dictionary
(large print edition)
Young Readers' Thesaurus
(large print edition)

For further information or a free brochure, please contact us at:
Ulverscroft Large Print Books Ltd.,
The Green, Bradgate Road, Anstey,
Leicester, LE7 7FU, England.
Tel: (00 44) 0116 236 4325
Fax: (00 44) 0116 234 0205

Marshal Rance Toller is locking up a pair of troublemakers when Angie Sutter, a homesteader from a nearby valley, arrives with the news that her husband was murdered that morning. Whilst Rance has qualms about heading out into the frozen wasteland, leaving only an ageing deputy to stand guard, he accompanies Angie to her cabin — to find not only Jacob Sutter's body, but also that of his neighbour, slain by the same weapon. Meanwhile, back at the jailhouse, the deputy is dead and the prisoners gone . . .

REBEL RAIDERS

John Dyson

A gang of former Confederate soldiers is robbing and killing its way across Kansas. Novice lawman Cass Clacy is sent out after them, but what chance does he have of outgunning such experienced fighters? When Sheriff Jim Clarke joins Cass in the chase, his main aim is a share of the reward. Together they penetrate deep into the heart of the Indian Nations, where Cass falls under the spell of the lovely Audrey — but can he save her from the clutches of the dangerous Josiah Baines?

THE COMANCHE FIGHTS AGAIN

D. M. Harrison

Mitch Bayfield, known as 'Broke', was kidnapped and raised as a Comanche. When, many years later, he looks for his kin, he finds himself unable to settle in either world and turns his back on them all. He is determined, however, to return and liberate Little Bluestem, another white captive. The two of them flee, with the Comanche hot on their trail — but they are about to tangle with a ruthless gang of bank robbers . . .

THE PRISONER OF GUN HILL

Owen G. Irons

When Luke Walsh falls for the beautiful Dee Dee Bright, he makes the biggest mistake of his young life. After she tricks him into killing the marshal of Tucson, Arizona, there is nothing for it but to take to the desert. But when his horse founders, he finds himself afoot and alone on the plain. Picked up by a passing wagon, he is set to work as slave labour in the Gun Hill gold mine — the remote outpost harbouring a nest of dangerous outlaws . . .